Absent from Class

Books by Grace Zolla Protano

As Long As You Can See the Clock, You're Okay

Absent from Class

A story of teacher burnout

Grace Zolla Protano

ProPress Books
Massapequa, New York

ProPress Books, Inc.
Massapequa, New York
http://www.propressbooks.net

ISBN 978-0-9845197-0-5

PRINTED IN THE UNITED STATES OF AMERICA

For Nick who supports me in everything I do

Acknowledgements

For my husband Nick who is always by my side cheering me on. His encouragement and unyielding faith in me made this work a joy.

Thank you to my good friend and colleague Russ Cera, author of *Cry Wolf, Cry,* for his literary input, writing skill and sense of humor.

To my daughters and my grandchildren for their enthusiasm to see this work to the end.

Tanti baci to my cousin Mari, my best fan.

ODE TO MY COLLEAGUES
On Grass

From afar it is simply a verdant ocean on a windy day
(Perhaps singing to Lycidas).

Close up it could be Green Knights
Daring us to cut their heads off.

Ceremoniously, we mow the lawn
And give the screw to Milton and Whomever.

— GZP

Chapter 1

Literature and its allusions were the only way Ceci McKinney could cope. It was grown-up make-believe. Sometimes even she couldn't tell the characters from herself.

Ceci told everyone she always wanted to be a teacher when in actuality she was afraid of speaking in front of a group. Though Vassar-educated, she was still inhibited by her speech quality. Hers was the regional tongue of South Brooklyn in the 50s mixed with the broken English patterns of Sicilian-born parents whose inflections in their speech influenced the way she spoke.

"How come you talk funny?" her students would ask. Rotten kids. She always hated when these upper middle-class kids said that to her. They never sensed that it embarrassed her. How could they? She was a superb actress.

She hated the first day of class. That was the day the kids—a group of individuals who outnumbered her and who embraced mob mentality—ganged up and tried to see how fast they could size up the teacher and determine how much they could get away with. So unfair. The teacher didn't know any of these people and these *hormones with legs* knew that. They had the advantage and capitalized on it. Just give her one week—and a seating chart—and she would get her revenge.

This year she was determined to get even more clever. She put the kids in alphabetical order and took a picture of the class. They thought it very dippy—and so did she—but she did it anyway, for survival's sake. The strategy didn't work because she couldn't remember a damn face the next day. Hey, give a teacher a break, she thought. There would be a hundred faces to memorize. That's if the district cooperated and put a cap on the number of students in each class. She normally couldn't remember who was who, so what was the point? She did, however, go through the usual teacher motions.

"Fill out the index card with the following info..."

"Does spelling count," a student asked.

"Yes, it does."

"Do we have to write in ink?"

"Yes, you do."

"Do we have to write in complete sentences?"

Realizing that this was going to be a very long year, she answered as gently as she could,

"Yes, dear, in complete sentences. Well, no, not when you're writing your first and last names." She was determined to get through this.

"Okay now. Put in your parents' names. Yes, sometimes the last name is different from yours." In this generation, she thought, the names always seem to be different.

She wanted to make the kids feel comfortable. "My own children had a different surname from mine," she lied for those students who looked embarrassed.

"When the students asked me, 'how come your daughter's name is different from yours?' I used to answer, 'because she is married.'"

"Wow, weren't you ticked off at her?" a future Mensa applicant would say.

"Sure. She is only twelve and her husband is younger." The students didn't know what to make of Ceci. They didn't ridicule her—not yet, anyway.

Ceci felt her head begin to ache and checked the 24-inch school clock which looked like it had been designed for the movie, *High Noon*. Gary Cooper, please walk in here now. It is only 10 am. A few more periods to go. And she really didn't care what these kids did on their summer vacations and didn't relish reading about them. She just needed the time to pass to get herself into the routine of school.

She couldn't believe she had 120 students. She filled out the student name cards, put them in alphabetical order in the seating charts and decided that it was all the work she would do on day one.

The second day would be better. They'd sit in their seats bored to death, daring her to try to teach them. No problem. She would distribute *Great Expectations* and instruct them to copy the list of vocabulary words for chapter one. Instant silence would follow by a gasp of disbelief.

They'd leave the classroom and complain to each other. Whew. She'd get through another day. As the days passed, she'd be less strict and they would either think they made a mistake in believing she was a witch or they would think they chiseled her down to the size they needed to throw imaginary airplanes at her.

Chapter 2

It was very early in the school year, and Ceci was already exhausted. Shoulders slouched, she walked into her house. A tall, slim man dressed in khaki Dockers and black polo shirt greeted her.

"Hey, Hon," Tim said.

"Hi." Was she the same person as one hour ago? Did she still enjoy humanity? She dropped her briefcase stuffed with what-did-you-do-over-the-summer-vacation papers that she was not going to read and let her coat fall naturally from her arms onto the recliner.

She could easily get to the top shelf, but she was too tired to stand on tippy-toe.

"Hey, Luv, could you get that glass for me?" she said. Tim reached up and gave her the Anchor Hocking stem glass. She felt pampered when she drank her $1 glass of sangria from her $1 Save-Mart glass. She agreed with him that she should drink more sophisticated wine.

She believed sangria was the wine of the pseudo-intellectuals of the 70s who were still reading *Jonathan Livingston Seagull* and thinking metaphysically about the meaning of anything. Actually, she liked that book and taught it to her remedial students. She always liked the irony in that. She would tell the group in her best seagull voice,

"The trick, Fletcher, is that we are trying to overcome our limitations, in order, patiently. We don't tackle flying through rock until a little later in the program." To the 70s reading public, this book was cult-like. She taught it—much to the chagrin of the administration—as a Christian-Judeo piece. She even taught that the initial of the protagonist symbolized Jesus. She had fun with it. She related the blue and white book cover to the Blessed Virgin Mary and her Renaissance-depicted robes of the same colors.

She got an especial kick out of liking sangria. It was as if she were slapping the faces of all wine connoisseurs, specifically Poe's Montresor and Fortunato from *The Cask of Amontillado.* She questioned Fortunato and was not afraid of being walled in by any psycho like Montresor. Ceci was the envious Montresor. She was the mason Fortunato. She was Poe, the author people feared.

She looked in the mirror. Today, she was a character in William Faulkner's "A Rose for Emily" and resembled Miss Emily Grierson with her steel gray hair. Ceci hoped she had plucked out all her own steel gray hair.

She warmed up the dinner she had prepared the day before and was grateful for being Italian and cooking lots of pasta and sauce on Sundays.

"Tim, did my mother call?"

"Your mother always calls."

"You really had to say that, right?"

"I really had to say that because your mother always calls."

Ceci got up from the table and Tim tried to hold her down. She pushed aside his hand from her shoulder and went into the living room.

"I'm sorry," he said.

"No, you're not."

"It's just that…"

"Well, if you were working like regular people, you wouldn't be home this early to answer the phone. You are not needed here."

He chose not to respond. Ceci wanted to feel bad, but she didn't. She knew how frustrated he was. She knew he preferred working from his office at the Center. It certainly would make their lives less stressful—for him at least—because he wouldn't have to be home before her and wouldn't be there as she walked in tired and, as always, very tense. Whenever he hit the sensitive nerve of her mother, all Ceci's defenses were bared and she got mean.

"Want to go for a walk?" he tried. "The kids are doing their homework—a miracle, I know—and we could break away for a half hour."

"No. Don't feel like it," she said.

"Come on," he said and tugged at her arm.

"Just read the paper. Hey, I have an idea. Maybe the want ads might suggest something productive to do. After all, you *are* home most of the day."

There was no stopping her and he knew he should just leave the room. There would be a fight and he was also very tired. Ceci could do that to a person.

She knew very well why he was tired.

James came bounding down the stairs. Ceci always wondered if her fourteen-year-old son knew there were thirteen steps to a flight instead of the five or six steps he used both going up and coming down.

"Really can't talk now, Mom," he said. "Got a lot to do. I'm going to take a shower, hit the books and turn in."

"Okay, Jimmy," she said. His long legs only needed five steps.

"Is it possible for you to slow down?" said his older sister moving aside in time to avoid collision on the landing.

"Perhaps," he said, "if you could appreciate school and all it has to offer as I do…"

"Perhaps," she said, "you can screw yourself." Barely acknowledging her mother, Jaime said, "See ya later."

"Where are you going? You have school tomorrow."

"Out. Bye."

Ceci knew there was no use trying to rein in her daughter. She would be graduating high school in June, was doing well and was basically a good kid—at least Ceci thought so, but she never told Jaime. Strong-willed and beautiful, Jaime used this combination to her advantage and it frightened Ceci.

James was still manageable and a much more pensive boy who really did enjoy learning. Usually in the world-basically-bores-me mode, Jimmy knew his tall athletic physique, short-cropped bronze-colored hair and almond-shaped eyes enticed the girls. They loved his long sideburns and his aloofness delighted them. He was in all honors classes and maintained a 97 average. If he was glum at times, it was accepted.

"That guy is so hot and he's a *genius*," the girls would say, allowing him to be any way he wanted.

Ceci went into the living room, pushed aside her coat and dumped herself into the worn black leather recliner. She liked the squishy sound it made. It seemed to be just as exhausted as she. Cushion suspiring with the sound of relaxation, it would make a good commercial for the See Ceci Sit Comfort Lounge Company.

"Got to get this thing fixed," she said aloud. "Maybe lose a few pounds. Probably cheaper and easier to buy a new one." The whole unit shook when she plopped into it.

"Everybody says things like that," she said, "but do people really buy a new one when things do not work? Or do they just live with broken things? How about when people break? Are broken people tolerated and endured? Does everyone forgive broken people?" She didn't, that's for sure. She decided to feel kind to Tim, a rare feeling. She forced a smile and said,

"Anything good on TV tonight?"

"Whatever you want, I want," he said.

At this point, he didn't care that much, but he was glad she was talking to him. She knew he didn't mean it and she called a truce.

Chapter 3

Ceci always began her Back to School Night speech with the same routine.

"If you promise not to believe anything your kids have said about me, I promise not to believe anything they've said about you." She had been teaching for so long, she wondered why she still got jittery and needed to hear the parents laugh at her jokes.

She told them of her determination, her credo, to teach the kids in spite of themselves. They would be reading *Great Expectations, Romeo and Juliet* and her favorite, *The Odyssey.*

"Now I am *sure* we are reading good stuff. You are making the same frowns as your cherubs." She was teaching an adult night class, she thought. She took out her chalk holder, loaded it and listed on the board the grammar to be covered. She made sure she screeched the chalk and smiled as she did when she teased her day classes.

"Oh, don't worry. You don't have to learn any of this garbage. Your kids don't worry, either." The parents laughed in unison.

"I heard you," she said pivoting to face them. She was the entertainer and she controlled them. If only this attitude lasted throughout the year. She hated calls from parents. She had to be "teacherish" and she wasn't.

What or who decided what went into *her* brain? Who entertained her, made her laugh, but cared so much for her that she learned of life without realizing it. Who? Her brother Alan, that's who. He was her food; he was her drink; he was her soul—before she tried to destroy it. What made him more special than anyone else? He didn't demand that privilege, that precious right that Ceci willingly gave him. He never saw her in a classroom and she wondered what he would think of her performance.

Unlike Ceci, Alan never needed to perform. She remembered when they were kids. Alan never internalized or believed anything she said to him when she was being the bratty kid she eventually admitted she was.

"You are the worst brother in the world."

"How could anybody live with such a rotten brother?"

"I wish Mommy never had you."

How, then, could she be expected to think that kids were any different in this generation? Maybe that's why she found it so easy to relate to them. Was it because she was really a kid? Could it be that was the only time in her existence that she liked herself, that she was actually happy? When her brother was in her life, he contributed to it, giving her the material with which to build something worthwhile. He neither criticized nor tried to mop us whatever mess she made. And mess, she made. Big time.

Chapter 4

She didn't tell her students that she had finished her memoir of growing up in Brooklyn in the 50s. If she shared it with them, they would figure out how old she was and they would know what a brat she had been as a kid. After convincing them that their generation was so different from the perfectly-behaved kids who lived in her own generation, she would have a hard time separating their Mrs. Ceci McKinney from smart-ass Ceci Scarpelli of the memoir. She enjoyed the sarcasm and bantering between her and her students. If they met Ceci Scarpelli, Mrs. McKinney would become transparent and lose credibility that she had this innate ability to control and maintain her position with them. In actuality, their classroom behavior was just a throwback to when she was their age. Their being aware of this wouldn't do at all.

These kids mirrored Ceci and her childhood friends. Maybe they had a little more money and more notches of playdates on their belts. Playdates. What were they? They weren't around in Brooklyn in the 50s. You just went outside. That was the playdate with whomever. You didn't know whom you were going to play with until you jumped down the two steps of the stoop and looked up and down the block. And you couldn't be late because of that damn Williamsburgh Bank clock tower in downtown Brooklyn. It was 512' of monolithic honesty looming in the distance keeping us kids rooted in time and place.

"Come in at 5:30. We're eating at 6. Don't be late," Gilda Scarpelli would say. It didn't matter if Ceci was in the middle of a great game of punchball. Ceci would end the game at 5:55 in order to make it up the two flights of stairs, two by two. No time to wash up. Her mother wouldn't notice if Ceci flew past her brother Alan and sat down, holding fork and spoon standing on their ends, prisoner style, pretending to demand to eat because she had been waiting sooo long. Her brother, however, would not allow this charade.

"I am not eating," Alan would say, "while looking at those grimy hands of hers."

"Then don't look or don't eat." Ceci's flippant remark got no points on the Smartass Meter because her mother was now alerted, eyes staring at Ceci as she'd drag to the kitchen sink and the soap dish.

"I hate you," she'd mouth to Alan, "and I always will, I swear."

He'd wink and whisper, "No, you won't, Sis, I swear."

And he was right.

Mrs. McKinney needed the class' attention.

"Okay, gang. Settle down. Settle down. Everything off your desks." Looking up together, they groaned, "Are we having a test?"

Ceci just preferred clean desks, test or no test.

"But we only had to look up the vocabulary words from *Great Expectations,*" they reminded her. Instead of using the first days of class strategy to get them back into school thinking mode, she needed to be the tough teacher who meant business. One of these days, she *would* give them an exam. After all, they did look up the vocabulary words. It was the least she could do.

"Take out your homework," she said, making sure she had her gradebook opened as she walked around, entering an imaginary mark. She had no idea who the kids were and it would be a while until she had even an inkling. She methodically put invisible checks on no names. She usually told the kids of this ruse sometime in June when she trusted them *not* to throw anything at her. She ran the risk of this ploy being discovered the following year if she had anybody's sibling.

"Mrs. McKinney. You had my brother last year."

"Then he'd be my son," she said. The student looked at Ceci and didn't think he should laugh. One wasn't amused at teachers' jokes—silly as they may be—on the third day of school. It was not cool. Not at all. It would only be okay to go home and tell your parents how funny—or how dumb—your teacher was and relay any remarks she made. If the parent laughed, then the student knew that this teacher was going to be fun. But you *never* said that to anyone.

"We have a faculty meeting this afternoon," Margot reminded Ceci.

"In the first week of school?"

"You sound like the kids."

With hands on hips and one foot stomping, Ceci replied, "I do not!"

Chapter 5

Tim stopped warning Ceci to lock her car. She always had a nasty comeback when he did. She secretly flipped the bird to her unlocked car as she prepared to enter the school. She knew why she was unkind to Tim.

"Because he's there," she said in a British accent paraphrasing what George Mallory said when he was asked why he wanted to climb Mt. Everest. It bugged Ceci that Sir Edmund Hillary always got credit for the phrase. She would rather have uttered those words than reached the summit, anyway. It was a great line and Ceci loved great lines.

Now she thought of another of her favorite phrases that Henry David Thoreau most likely never said. The story went that when Thoreau was jailed for his civil disobedience in not paying some real estate taxes, Ralph Waldo Emerson visited him and said, "What are you doing in there?"

"The question is: what are you doing *out* there?" Thoreau was said to have replied.

Most English professors, specifically the self-appointed Internet Snopesians, agreed he never said any such thing. It didn't matter. If Emerson had reached into his tight ecru breeches for a wad of ready cash to bail out Thoreau, Thoreau would have known that it was nothing more than an ostentatious transcendental gesture because Thoreau's trusty aunt would be bailing him out in order to make him more civilly obedient. He probably didn't mind the attention the jail time gave him, but preferred living on Emerson's Walden Pond pretending he was simplifying his life while his mother and a score of neighbors visited him regularly bringing him baked goodies. And Emerson just a pond's pebble throw away was added security.

At least that's what Ceci thought.

It was the annual Welcome Back Teachers meeting and School Superintendent Pasquale Abramson approached the dais to address the not-so-enthusiastic audience who were just beginning to relax by the end of August. Ceci liked the incongruity of his name. She could just hear the grandmothers talking:

"So, Mrs. Bacciagalupo. Have I got a boy for your daughter! He's handsome, he's smart and he'll make good money some day. Trust me."

"Sure. Sure, Mrs. Abramson. Only please, one thing. Can they name their first son Pasquale after my papa, may he rest in peace," she said crossing herself invoking the Holy Trinity.

"Pasquale, Shmasquale…who cares? I don't care. As long as they're happy. As long as they're happy that's what I say."

"Yes, yes," said Mrs. Bacciagalupo, "and we will make sure of that. We certainly will."

"I'm not the type to interfere, but…"

"Neither am I," agreed Mrs. Bacciagalupo.

Ceci knew Pat Abramson couldn't possibly be happy greeting the faculty and trusting they had a restful summer. He hoped they were prepared to work with a dynamic staff and introduced them to the thirteen new members of the teaching profession.

"I know you will be absolutely impressed with the credentials of these thirteen fine new colleagues," said the Superintendent. He mentioned the colleges they graduated from and none of the older faculty really gave a rat's rear.

"Very prophetic number to join our staff," Ceci said to anybody.

Two of the eager-to-transform-the-educational-world were English teachers assigned to Ceci's building and department. Both probably wouldn't admit to her that they knew diddly about grammar and wouldn't ask for help, either. Of course, she would notice the deficiency after just one checking of their planbooks. With a little grinding of her teeth, she would initial the books in approval.

"No, predicate adjectives do not follow action verbs. Yes, subordinators do introduce dependent clauses. An adverbial phrase *is* a prepositional phrase. Say, why don't you stop by on your prep period and I can go over any exercises you are not sure of."

They'd act blasé about agreeing to come, but Ceci knew they were anxious to. They couldn't admit it to the chairperson lest she think they didn't know grammar. They didn't and Ceci knew they didn't because that's the way she had been when she began her career. Only things were different then.

She used to ask for help.

She complained as loudly as anybody did—even though she was chairperson and technically considered an administrator. Everybody knew that administrators accepted everything with grace. Wasn't she supposed to have a certain élan that rose above the average lowly teacher?

"Screw élan," she said aloud, again to anyone. She never sought the job of chairperson. The district didn't want Naomi Singer to head the department even though she was probably more qualified and the other members were too young (even though they went to impressive colleges.)

Most teachers hated Naomi Singer, but none more than Ceci did. It was easy to. Naomi bragged about her home in Montauk, Long Island. She bragged about her BMW with the vanity plates *Nee's Bee*. She was sure she had an image others envied. Naomi would turn in her mother for taking extra napkins home from a diner if it made Naomi look admirably ethical. Financially comfortable at 56, Naomi was still single and lived with her mother as long as, Ceci presumed, the mother obeyed the law.

"That bitch has it made," the teachers would say, "No extra expenses. No kids to drive her crazy. Nobody to nag her and demand she cook for them. Of course, she can have anything she wants."

Except Tim. Naomi wanted Tim, but then again, *everybody* wanted Tim with his light auburn hair, side parted, which added a Rockwellian innocence to a fine-featured face that so appealed to women.

"Where did you get those gorgeous eyes?" she would ask him at every holiday party. "What do I have to do to get you to look my way?"

"Wear a bag over your head," Ceci would answer.

The school district couldn't use the term *Christmas* parties. Not politically correct. Among themselves, though, the teachers said *Christmas* instead of *holiday*. Nothing could be in writing because writing made things permanent. Ideas and emotions could not be put on paper—unless you were a good writer. And Ceci was.

Wasted talent, that's for sure. What good was writing a memoir if you weren't sure if you'd let anybody read it? Ceci's manuscript was written with ink of blood that came out as she sliced through the memory of her life. How could you pierce your mind and not expect blood to leak out? The advantage to writing with dripping blood was that it made a pretty ink—at least while it was fresh. The memoir was her red badge of courage. But to whom could she show it? Her students so they could laugh at her? Her colleagues so they would know that she was "all talk" when she sternly gave her opinion about things? She would have to wait until she retired at the end of the year before she would allow herself to bleed out. But she wanted someone to stroke the book now. She would have liked some accolades now.

Tim loved the memoir and teared up when he finished reading it. What kind of a guy cries when he reads a book, she thought, and forced herself *not* to see him in that light.

Then it would be too hard not to love him.

Chapter 6

Tracy, the tall brunette language signer, dragged in the table to be stored on the side of Ceci's room. The teacher aid Stephanie carried their briefcases, handbags and Marshall's backpack. Tracy was both signer for Marshall and interpreter for Stephanie. Marshall waited in the corridor howling in annoyance for being kept waiting in the wing for his grand entrance. The ever territorial Ceci watched as two strangers came into her classroom and rearranged the seating. First desk, first row was no longer as she had it.

Marshall Keller was wheeled in and guided to the empty area created by Tracy's desk shuffling. First row, first seat Marshall. Next to Marshall, Stephanie's chair with all her material in canvas totes on the floor to her right. To Marshall's right was his backpack in handy reach of his only viable limb. Stephanie dragged a chair for Tracy to the left of the teacher's desk and the whole entourage was ready for school. The rest of the students watched the free show and were thrilled that nine minutes of the period was spent.

Ceci had no idea what had just transpired. The Guidance Department wouldn't notify her until the next day that she would be getting Marshall Keller, a boy with cerebral palsy who was deaf, unable to speak, unable to walk and only had use of one arm.

Ceci was to learn later that Marshall could keep up with the rest of the students with his one hand and gaunt, but smiling, face which seemed to welcome each day. In practiced and methodical movements, his small stature could maneuver his motorized wheelchair, manage to fish out a piece of paper from his backpack and place the now-wrinkled sheet on the flip-aside mini desk of his wheelchair. Stephanie would help Marshall shape his hand and form it around his pen, periodically checking to make sure it didn't slip out of the minimal grip he had.

What his body lacked in physical strength, his facial expressions more than compensated. With a mother who made sure his tawny hair was neatly trimmed and styled, Marshall enjoyed the generous compliments he received from classmates for his oversized designer sweatsuits and Adidas sneakers that never got soiled. Decked out in apparel his classmates approved, Marshall waited to be taught. He would muster a guttural laugh when pleased. He would grunt in displeasure if Ceci or anyone within hearing of 100 miles didn't acknowledge his presence.

Ceci was angry at not being informed that this physically-challenged boy was her new student. It was her last year of teaching and she had planned on a smooth entry into retirement—nothing new in her curriculum, nothing new to read in preparation of teaching ninth grade English. She merely wanted to take out her planbook to pretend, as she always did, that she was consulting it to see what they would be doing each day.

Each academic year was the same. The first quarter she would cover the works of Charles Dickens, the second William Shakespeare, the third the poet Homer, and the last quarter a series of short stories of authors she particularly favored. Nobody wanted to work in the last quarter of the year, so she needed to reduce the pressure on the students, as well as on herself. Short stories allowed for a beginning and an end to the material covered each day. If a student dozed through the lesson, there would be a clean, new one the next day. The short story unit exams could be passed even if a student hadn't read one or two of the twelve stories covered in the quarter. Everything was neatly planned out and there was no need for a traditional planbook. She kept it because of the Mount Everest thing. She was chairperson, so nobody would be checking hers, except maybe Naomi Singer when she sneaked into Ceci's room and rummaged through her desk looking for material she could pilfer and claim as her own.

Rationalizing stealing another teacher's material, Naomi would say, "I should think as chairperson, however ineffective, Mrs. McKinney would let the rest of the department see 'how it's done,' if, in fact, it *is* done."

Ceci knew these nighttime forays had taken place. Naomi and the head custodian Jerry had been paramours for eighteen years enjoying the supply walk-in closet that also supplied the two with supine satisfaction.

For the enjoyment of the rest of the faculty, Ceci regularly reminded Naomi of the dangers of trying to spy on a person of Sicilian descent. In the morning, there would be some Italian item—the latest being a robust ceramic gondolier with his head broken and the shards spread across Naomi's desk calendar. Then it was even harder to look at Naomi's face with its dark leather-like skin, compliments of her summers under the Aruba sun. Naomi happy was a fright to look at; Naomi angry was a guaranteed nightmare.

Ceci's papers had been submitted and the news of her planned retirement flashed throughout the building. Naomi salivated at the hope of getting Ceci's job. Although not totally successful, Ceci did try to overlook the antics of Naomi. She wanted to complete her last year of teaching uneventfully.

Until Marshall showed up. And showed up he did! Steel wheelchair wheels banged into the archway to room 117; backpack pulled in and dumped beside him; desks dragged aside to make room for the "king" as she would tease him after he got used to her. Or was it after she got used to him? It agreeably surprised her how teenaged students—normally those monsters whose object in life was to torment the teacher—could accept and adapt so effortlessly. And they did with Marshall breaking into their English class.

It was on a Wednesday and he did not wait for Tracy to interpret what he wanted to say. Bobbing his head uncontrollably, he roared in excitement. Ceci looked at Tracy for a translation.

"It's his birthday in two days. He is reminding you and every other person whose attention he can get."

Ceci smiled at him and nodded emphatically and uselessly spoke loudly to Marshall.

"Okay," Ceci said. "Good." At first, it was difficult and a bit uncomfortable connecting with Marshall. She didn't like feeling the way the kids sometimes did—that some of what he had could rub off on her. But that feeling would change later on for Ceci.

The next day His Majesty Marshall Keller made his same grand entrance, but this time held up the gnarled index finger of his only good hand.

"I know. I know," Ceci said. "One more day until your birthday." She felt a little nervous at this thought. Ceci would have to engage this boy in a classroom rite that she gave all the students on their birthdays—a group song and a snack. It was an ordinary celebration occurrence in her classroom, but Marshall was not an ordinary kid.

"I will bring in some donuts," Ceci said to Tracy, "and a special chocolate iced cupcake for Marshall. We'll put number candles on it. How old will he be?"

"Eighteen," Tracy replied understanding Ceci's wonder as kids in the ninth grade usually celebrated their fourteenth or fifteenth birthdays.

The regal day arrived and the period bell pealed in proclamation. Marshall, stately donning his Burger King crown—compliments of Stephanie—fit the title Ceci always playfully assigned to him and came rolling in. Beaming, his uneven teeth bared to expose happiness the only way he knew how. His grunts of pleasure were rather loud and Stephanie and Tracy motioned for him to lighten them a bit. He made a grotesque facial expression to apologize for feeling giddy, but now it was he who was teasing.

"Oops," he would have said if he could, "sorry, but it *is* my birthday, you know."

Ceci prepared to open the box of donuts to distribute when she was interrupted. As all the students came to the front of the room, she was surprised that they would usurp the teacher-planned activity. All together, they gathered round Marshall, faced him and waited until everyone was ready to sign.

They waved the flat of their hands to bring happiness up from their stomachs. Middle fingers touched chins to hearts. Index fingers pointed to Marshall who had taken out his imaginary baton and led the chorus of his young classmates as they signed happy birthday to him. They finished with each touching his own heart.

As hard as she tried, Ceci could not stop the tears and she fumbled for the tissue box reserved for her students who usually stood by her desk, blew their noses and many times missed the trash can. There were no more tissues left and no place to hide her face. Fortunately, the door was close to the activity. She could allow her emotions to take over in the privacy of an empty school corridor.

"This is not the way a kid should celebrate his eighteenth birthday," she said to the concerned principal who approached her, "and certainly not in silence while your classmates are singing happy birthday in sign language."

"He heard them, loud and clear," the principal said. As soon as she was composed, she reentered the classroom as Marshall howled in laughter and waved her to her seat to have a donut.

"They're yummy," he must have said to her, "try one." She motioned to him to blow out the unlit numbers one and eight candles. She pointed to the gooey chocolate cupcake she made for him and she thought she saw his expression change slightly. No, he motioned, and turned to his classmates as they indulged in their sweets.

It was not until later on in the faculty room that Ceci spoke to Tracy.

"What a great time Marshall had."

"Yes. Thank you for allowing that, Mrs. McKinney."

"I guess he was too excited to eat his cupcake."

Tracy's face told Ceci that there was something she didn't see.

"He will eat it later on when he is alone—with just Stephanie and me," Tracy said.

Ceci always believed she was very smart and how in tune she was with anyone around her. So many years in the classroom and working with more than 2000 kids on individual bases resulted in giving her teacher eyes and ears, teacher sonar, radar, whatever to understand the human condition even if the signs were not obvious to the people themselves. She knew everything. She knew all the signs.

But she never noticed Marshall's embarrassment at the thought of eating a chocolate-iced cupcake in front of the class.

Chapter 7

It was Tim's night to be with the guys. She always hated when husbands said that. *Out with the guys*. They'd bowl a few games and then go out for a beer. How utterly mundane. She didn't think Tim even liked bowling and he only drank red Zinfandel.

"Do you honestly find those men and their conversation stimulating?"

"Matter of fact I do."

"Maybe when all of you were kids, but why now? Your careers are…different. You are a psychiatrist, for God's sake. Does any of them actually *have* a career? You can't talk shop, that's for sure," she said.

That was precisely the reason Tim spent time with these Brooklyn friends from a life long passed. He didn't have to talk patients. He didn't have to talk about Ceci. He didn't have to analyze *anything*. And he wasn't expected to.

"No, you bowl clean-up," Tim said. "Me, I'm no good under pressure.

"Okay," Ralph said, "but some time you gotta try it." Tim always smiled when Ralph suggested Tim bowl last for the team. He knew Ralph treasured being in this coveted position of being trusted and depended upon. Sometimes Tim's life was a bowling game, and he had no choice but to bowl clean-up. And he was getting tired of it.

"Go, Ralphie Boy," he'd say in his best impression of Art Carney as Ed Norton. Tommy and Tony always belly-laughed. It infuriated Ceci that Tim's boyhood pal Ralph was a Metro bus driver as the character Ralph Kramden in the Jackie Gleason 1950s hit TV series, *The Honeymooners*. Tim found the whole coincidence even more comical because it annoyed Ceci so much.

Ceci was in the mood for some hamburgers. She avoided going to Burger King lest she think of Marshall and his bobbing head with the cardboard gold crown shaking upon it.

"Uneasy lies the head that wears a crown," she thought. Good old Willy S. That bard always knew what he was talking about.

She saw the entrance to McDonald's and drove into the exit. Another Mt. Everest thing. Today she would eat two cheeseburgers and a large order of fries *before* going home. Tim had planned to cook for her and the kids and she was not going to tell them that she had already eaten at McDonald's. She couldn't miss the opportunity to assume martyr role on his night when he would spend a few hours away from her with Jackie Gleason disguised as Ralph, Tim's friend.

"No, Timmy honey. I am too stressed to eat. You go on out. I'll be fine." She wished guilt tactics worked like they used to when they were first married. Only then he never cared to go out without her. As a matter of fact, nothing was like when they were first married.

She stuffed the empty soda cup into the McDonald's bag and had a difficult time bending the straw to fit under the plastic cup cover that never prevented any soda from spilling. She scrunched up the bag as small as she could and shoved it under the driver's seat. She would throw it out tomorrow along with the bag from last week.

Chapter 8

Jimmy never remembered to turn off the TV. Ceci thought her son was getting too tall for his bed and wondered if they made single beds longer, like single kings. Hmmm, single kings.

Never would have happened in England, she thought. What about their precious notion of the heir? Can't have an heir if a single king can't heir anybody. Doesn't matter how his lady was treated. Look at Henry and what happened to his ladies when they didn't cooperate and heir him many boys.

To heir is human, unless you're divine. She loved how witty she was. She really couldn't be too disparaging on those who wanted sons. She wanted only sons and never understood why Tim didn't care what they had.

"We have the perfect family," Tim would joke. "Mother, father, a boy, a girl and a dog. That's what our family is. Perfect." He certainly couldn't believe that, she thought—at least not after the first few years of marriage.

"Jimmy, come on. Get up. You are never going to be able to sleep through the night. Aren't you a tad too old for naps?"

"What's the diff? I'm up all night, anyway."

He did not in fact sleep and that's why he needed his naps. She tried to discourage him from sleeping in the day, but it made no difference to his inability to sleep at night. The night was when he tried to solve all his problems; the night was his personal world inhabited by one person.

Jimmy turned over in bed and pulled the covers higher over his face to keep out both the light and Ceci. He was definitely growing up. At an even 6', he already surpassed Tim in height and build.

Jimmy was not as handsome as Tim because Tim, at 57, was still a looker. Tim's blue eyes and boyishly thick hair could turn heads. The bounce in his walk had deflated, that's true, but his slim physique and more than friendly demeanor took on a Richard Cory air that could flutter pulses as he walked. Except Ceci's.

He stopped feeling for her. He stopped enjoying her. And he stopped rooting for her. Yes, she was bitchy, but she hadn't always been that way. Sometimes people were forced into bitchdom, she thought, by the very charges who complain. That was Ceci's credo and she was religious about believing it in her treatment of her husband, her children, her colleagues and her students. Her heart was easily battered and she must protect it even though no one believed that it could actually be damaged.

She knew Tim felt the way he did. He lived in Scarlet O'Hara mode. Tomorrow would be a better day. But the tomorrows *weren't* better days. With the exception of Ceci, he had just about kept all his other relationships intact. His kids adored him; his parents and adult siblings respected him. Everybody thought he was *the man.* Well, almost everybody. Tim knew how Ceci felt and Ceci knew that he knew it. They both, in their own ways, wondered what could be done.

Divorce would be easy, but it was out of the question.

Chapter 9

It wasn't her fault that she misplaced the mortgage money. When she was upset, she reasoned, she didn't remember squat. Retrace your steps. What were you doing last? Go back to where you were when last you had it. She knew those suggestions by heart.

$2900. Sure, it wasn't the end of the world. She could withdraw that much from the savings account and cover the mortgage, but that wasn't the point. She hated when she did stupid things. She would laugh at this one day, she reasoned. But not today. Frantically, she used her hands to machete through the jungle of papers she had on her desk, on the floor near her desk, in the wastebasket.

Hours later she found the money. "I put it in a drawer I never use," she told Tim.

"Not true anymore," he said.

She would have laughed if someone else had said that. *She* certainly would have said it to someone else. Why didn't she find Tim funny? She used to.

As her students would say, she was getting "old timers' disease." She liked that phrase better than Alzheimer's. Old timers' disease had a nice gentle charm to it and not the illness she feared most.

She needed to take her mind off things.

"Not a difficult task given there is such a small arena within which to work," her brother Alan would say. Very funny, Alice. This reference, also from *The Honeymooners*, made her laugh. "Pow, to the moon," they would have said at the same time, joined pinky fingers and hugged. She thought of her brother very often. What nerve he had to die before her. Oh, he looked smooth all right holding his lit cigarette between thumb and forefinger cupped in his slowly swinging hand as he walked. In the 50s life was so simple, she thought. Lung cancer? Nah, that was for old people. And anyway cigarette smoking didn't cause cancer. Anybody knew that.

Alan had been the same age as Tim and she couldn't avoid comparing them. Alan was the only one Ceci could really talk to and how she wished she could tell him about the crap she wallowed in daily. He always knew the right thing to say. Tim tried to be like Alan, but he couldn't. Sometimes that made her angry; sometimes she liked it.

Ceci laughed at herself for having named her kids James and Jaime.

"The third kid will be Jimmy-Jaime. How does that sound, Alan?"

"You could always run it by Mom, ya know."

"Oh that's a good idea. First I'd like to set my hair on fire and walk on nails to get in practice for our chat."

The only James she knew she didn't even like. Funny how hard it was to find a name for a child without thinking of a person you knew with the same name. If you liked the person, then the name was fine. If you didn't like the person, you knew you would have a hard time calling your child by that name. Take Adolph. You wouldn't name a child Adolph.

"On the other hand, the name Hitler is okay," a student commented trying to emulate Ceci's wit. She knew the student was trying to be funny. The phrase *was* funny for funny phrases' sake. But that was it.

"Whoa now. I know you are being cute. You don't want to minimize the suffering and death of millions caused by that monster, do you? Nothing at all funny about it."

Feeling embarrassed at the sudden seriousness of Ceci's face, the student flushed. "I...I didn't mean that Mrs. McKinney."

"I know you didn't. Some of my best friends are Jewish," she said.

She also hated when people used clichés, even though some of her best friends *were* Jewish. In fact, her very best friend was Jewish and when she told this same story to Margot, she laughed. Just Ceci's normal sarcasm.

"You are so lucky I am not prejudiced, you dago," Margot would say.

Ceci got into more trouble for what she considered funny than anyone else in the building. She wanted to change. It would have been nice to be thought of as a soft, sweet person. No one would ever have thought her kind and sensitive, so it was easier to playfully insult everyone.

She read somewhere that when people act the clown, they keep others controlled and at a distance. It was really simple: She made people laugh. They were out of her personal space while they were backing up and chuckling. They didn't approach her emotionally because they were enjoying the show. She could monitor how the situation was going. If they were laughing, they were not touching her. It worked all the time.

She had a wasteland of people wanting to comfort her, wanting to hug her. She was getting tired of working so hard at keeping people away. Nobody argued with her. Nobody asked her to stop entertaining them so she would be clear of any interactive obstructions. No roadblocks to prevent them from getting close. Most behaved themselves and kept away. Everybody was happy and nobody had to deal with Ceci. She was a witch with a capital b, they probably thought.

"What do you want, Jaime?"

"Oh, how utterly motherly of you,"

"You are normally a hundred miles away anyway," Ceci started.

"Why is that, I wonder?"

"What, are we reversing the psychology? You are too young, too inexperienced and too mild to be an opponent, my dear child."

"You always say I am unreachable. I am distant. I don't talk to you the way your friends' daughters talk to them. Can you not figure out why?"

"Here it comes," Ceci said looking at the ceiling the way her students did when she began her typical I-am-the-teacher-and-I-know-more-than-you speeches.

Exhaling loudly, Jaime got up and stood for a while staring at Ceci. Jaime began to walk away and returned as if to finish the sentence she was going to begin. She took a step toward Ceci as she unconsciously backed up. Jaime, noticing her mother's retreat, changed her mind and turned around and walked out of the room.

"Ha, living room," Jaime said. "What an ironic name for a room that contained a so-called mother and a daughter who wants to talk to her about filling in some gaps."

"I beg your pardon," said Ceci.

"Forget it. It's not important."

Can a mother fill in the gaps if the mother didn't think it was she who caused the gaps in the first place? Did it really matter who caused the gaps? Was a mother expected to know when there were gaps? Jaime thought so.

It annoyed Ceci that her own mother knew when something was wrong and knew when to call. Mother-Radar. Gilda knew the precise moment her daughter Ceci was in trouble and the phone would ring three minutes later.

"No, Mom. Everything's fine. Why do you call so many times? You know Timmy doesn't like it when we are eating and the phone rings. No, I won't shut off the ringer. Never know if it will be an important call. Yes, Mom, your calls are important. Just not necessary. I am fine, really."

"What is wrong? A mother knows," Gilda would say totally ignoring the explanation of Ceci who was, Gilda knew full well, in deep turmoil.

Chapter 10

Ceci wondered why anyone would name her child Clarence. It was a good enough name, but certainly not for this neighborhood with the Kyles, Brandons, Chloes, and Emmas. She wondered what the trend was when mothers originally named their kids. Was there a book of names that Jesus walked around with like Moses did the Ten Commandments? Was there a sermon on a Popular Children's Names Mount where He periodically read from a list and said,

"Okay, these are the names for the next two years. I'll be back in a couple to read the next batch."

If anyone veered off with an Andrew when it should have been a Zachary, there would be the wrath of You-Know-Who.

Ceci committed the sin and felt the wrath of Gilda. Ceci did not like the name Gilda. It scared her for some reason—the parent as well as the name. It always reminded her of Rapunzel or some Scandinavian lost kid with one long blond braided hair. Her mother had short black hair, but Ceci was always afraid she would wake up some day and find a different mother running her life. This time it would be one who looked like Peggy Wood from the 50s television show *I Remember Mama* (a great show if one could get past all the yas and Aunt Yennies.) It was the precursor, with a Norwegian accent, of the 70s *The Waltons*.

Couldn't put anything over on Mama. Shrewd old broad. And Lars. Good man, her husband. A shame he was bald. Alan had shocks of thick hair to make Lars yump ship to borrow some of Alan's locks. Then there was Nels. Ceci liked Nels' chubby cheeks and affable attitude. He always reminded her, though, of someone who wouldn't succeed at much. She guessed she had eight reasons (was it enough?) why actor Dick Van Patten, who played Nels, would never make it in Hollywood. She'd concede and give him credit for his popular television show of the 70's, *Eight is Enough.*

Clarence Gummajian was a goofy kid and a bit hygiene-challenged. Lanky at nearly 6', he would have been the envy of the other 14- and 15-year-olds if it hadn't been for his aversion to Irish Spring soap. He stole so many things in class that he was automatically under suspicion for anything that was missing. He could get away with taking someone's plastic Bic pen or Dubble Bubble gum, but when the board erasers were bulging out of a hand-me-down backpack...

Ceci loved Combos, those cheese-stuffed pretzel snacks. She kept them hidden in her drawer, but the students always knew where anything was. They also knew everything she did and could pin-point the very next dumb joke (as they described it) she would tell. She once gave the students a quiz and legitimately counted it. She said it was to test to see how observant they were. What college did she go to? How many brothers and sisters did she have? What was her dog's name? What was her favorite food?

The students couldn't remember the eight parts of speech, but they could remember any eight facts about her. It was fun to watch herself through her students' eyes.

- She tapped her watch face with her nails
- She looked at the clock more often than the kids did
- Whenever she was concentrating at her desk, she opened and closed the middle drawer
- She always wore something black on Mondays
- She laughed at her own jokes before the punch line
- She lost her keys daily
- She jammed the Xerox machine in the faculty room at least twice a week
- She caught kids chewing gum, even if they weren't

The class had been producing well for the quarter and Ceci decided to give them a treat—which was more for her. She told them she would select a class and allow some of the kids to be Mrs. McKinney for the period. Anything was allowed. A teacher had to have faith in the class and trust them not to be cruel. Ceci had no intention of picking her sixth period class because they didn't like her. Maybe it was because she didn't like them. Steven Temple being in that class solidified her feeling.

She waited until the end of the period to tell them.

"Tomorrow, we will see just how observant you really are. Observation and absorption go together." She was pretty sure that was true. It sounded true and profound and she was in a profound mood.

Chapter 11

Clarence Gummajian was chosen to be the person who would imitate Ceci. His was the most vigorous hand waving and his "pick me, pick me" the most convincing. She was a bit concerned at Clarence being selected because she had seen him between periods look a little too interested in her middle desk drawer.

"Clarence," she had screamed. "Don't ever, *ever*, go into my desk drawer again."

He looked guilty, but not sorry, she thought.

"I am going to let you imitate me today because I promised I would, but I am very, very disappointed in you."

He just looked at her, said nothing and left the room.

"An apology wouldn't hurt, young man." She strongly doubted that he would grow up to be an honorable man.

The criterion for winning the enviable role was answering correctly the questions about Ceci. Clarence couldn't pass an exam or quiz, either surprise or planned, but he knew everything about her. She wondered if that experiment showed that the students were rapt by everything she uttered in class or that she repeated the same thing over and over and over. She didn't think about this too long because she knew the answer. Jaime and Jimmy always complained that she would finish a story and immediately begin it again with the same enthusiasm as the first rendition. Clarence had been preparing for the show and was as anxious to perform as the students were to see Ceci roasted. He walked into the classroom.

"Do you have a tissue?" one of the students asked Clarence on cue.

"Tissue? I don't even know you." Barump bump. He sat at her desk.

"Okay class. Everything off your desks," which brought on classroom groans. "No test. Just wanted the desk clean," he said. "Oh did I tell you what happened when the two peanuts were walking in the park together? One was assaulted." Barump bump. He opened the middle desk drawer and took out a bag of Combos that he had planted there between periods earlier in the day. He opened the bag and began eating them.

"Ooh, I love these things. I love the pizza-flavored ones the best. Hmmm, I wonder if they are fattening," he said and searched the bag for the caloric content.

"Oh, who cares," he said and poured them in his mouth talking with his mouth full. He searched the room.

"If anybody has gum, shpitt it out," he said to the uncontrollably laughing class as they wiped away the rain of Combo crumbs he sprayed at them.

The class applauded at Clarence's stellar performance and he took his bow. He was proud of himself for making the class and Ceci laugh.

He never realized that she had forced her laugh to hide the shame she felt for scolding and accusing him earlier.

Chapter 12

She put down her briefcase, shoulder tote and lunch bag and stretched to reach into her mailbox in the teacher's cubby of the Alcmene High School general office.

"Is anybody ever going to fix this dangling name label?" Sure, she could do it herself, but why should she? That was not her job. She wondered if it would hold out until she retired at the end of June. It reminded her of the story "The Last Leaf," by O Henry.

Was she like the seriously-ill Johnsy from the story who would let herself die when the last leaf fell? Would the school administration behave like old Behrman, the failure in art, who finally painted his masterpiece for Johnsy—a leaf on the blank side of the adjoining brick house?

Fiction, she thought. Sappy fiction at that. Yet she always liked that story because she felt there was a secret understanding between her and William Sidney Porter. Maybe she would write her story called "The Last Label" and write under the pen name of O Ceci. It would be a story about the day she walked out of the district, out of her career, out of the lives of these kids. Was she a part of theirs? Were they a part of hers?

That teacher name label would surely fall to the ground. The night custodian would sweep it up along with the gum wrappers, hall passes the monitors never checked and See Me notes from the principal.

Ceci was beginning to feel melancholy very often, but she made sure she didn't show it. With her upbeat, perpetually affective Mary Poppins sing-songy voice, she could dupe just about anyone. She could make people laugh whenever she chose. What would she have thought if most of her subjects were aware of her game?

The possibility that people may have felt sorry for her never entered her thoughts because she couldn't deal with that. No emotional interaction was allowed.

Her brother Alan, if he only had lived, would be able to stop her in her humorous tracks and say, "Cut the crap, girl. Stop hurting. You look like an idiot when you grimace trying to force that laugh."

She was angry at Tim for no longer being able to tell when she was hurting and when she was pretending not to be hurting. She was angry that she couldn't tell him she understood and appreciated why he couldn't work anymore. She didn't have the luxury to allow herself to quit. She had a few more months until she would be eligible for the retirement incentive and her school pension would be enough to contribute much to the family's financial needs. She would retain free medical and Tim's proposed therapy for her would be paid for in full.

She couldn't help but think of Ken Kesey's *One Flew Over the Cuckoo's Nest* when Tim casually mentioned that

Electroshock Convulsive Therapy was making a quite comeback. She wondered if people ever really needed shock treatments instead of chemically-induced therapy with some serious talking to.

She always felt Holden Caulfield just needed a swift kick in his upscale Manhattan butt. That suggestion always got sneers from her students who thought of Holden with reverence. When she shared her opinion with the parents on Back to School Night, they all agreed that that technique most certainly would work on their own kids.

She was sure they didn't think that way when they, themselves, as teenagers read *Catcher in the Rye.*

Chapter 13

She lay on the unmade bed and tried to fluff up the already-fluffed-too-many-times pillow she had propped against the metal headboard. Why did she ever buy that thing? Every time she tried to sit up in bed, she would slide down it; every time she turned over in bed, part of the pillow would slip through the rounded ornamental scroll at the base of the headboard and eventually she would be sleeping on one quarter of the pillow which was now totally unfluffed.

She finally got herself in a relatively comfortable position and sighed when she realized that she was just lying there now unable to fall asleep. She would have to wait for a productive idea to come to her.

"Hey, Ma," Jimmy said as he slid past her room.

"Hello," she said, still trying to think of something to do so as not to waste the comfortable position she was finally in. To appear as though she was deep in creative thought, she casually crossed her ankles and folded her arms.

"Mom?"

"It only requires one hello to be acknowledged. We don't live in a mansion where we cannot communicate without shouting.

"Mom?"

She looked over at him and wondered at his not hearing her.

Jimmy walked closer to her and stood by the bed. He stared at her awhile and waited for a response. He was very much like Ceci was when she was young and would enter a room to find her father Gino reposing. If Gino were sleeping soundly, Ceci wouldn't nudge him to wake him but would simply stand beside him and wait until she saw steady breathing. Once, twice, three times. Better wait for the fourth. There. He was fine. She also did that to her children when they were in their cribs. Couldn't ever be too certain.

Her father would open his eyes in that way people can feel the presence of another near. She always heard of that phenomenon, but thought the person was on the brink of awakening and the presence was easier felt if the person was almost awake anyway. James stood there counting his mother's breaths in her feigned deep sleep. She wanted to jump up into a sitting position and scare the smarty pants off him.

Jimmy dragged a folding chair to the side of the bed and sat down next to her. He unzipped his backpack and pulled out his *Norton's English Anthology* and his spiral notebook and dumped them onto the bed beside her crossed ankles. He waited for her to awaken.

"Move over, Mom." She obeyed him and readjusted her comfort zone, pulling the pillow from under the headboard and repositioning it next to Tim's side, pushing his pillow onto the floor. After being hit by Tim's pillow, Goldie, the white and tan spitz mix, scampered away a few paces with the pillow following her. She slowly sniffed it and when she was satisfied there weren't any emotions left on it, trotted away. She did not leave the room, but made herself comfortable at the portal of the bedroom.

"Must be nice to be a dog, to be able to get comfortable in one second," she said, yawning and stretching.

James shifted onto the side of the bed, one leg on the mattress, the other on the floor. "Good morning. It's 3:30 in the afternoon. Didn't know you had the day off."

"I don't," she said. "Just cutting school."

"I can't stand him and never understand a blasted thing he writes," he said. Ceci always enjoyed the phrases he used. What 14-year-old kid said *blasted*? And he wasn't deliberately substituting it for the four-letter word popular with kids his age. And he didn't refrain from using the f word because he thought it was obscene. It just wasn't the word he was looking for.

"Blasted? Couldn't you think of a kid word?" she said laughing.

"The difference between the right word and the almost right word is the difference between lightning and the lightning bug," he said.

"Ah, long lives Mark Twain," she said making sure he knew she got the pun. "Who is it this time?" she asked.

"Ezra Pound. He's worse than James Joyce."

"Don't think you mean worse. Think you mean harder. And he isn't. James Joyce is worse," she said and they both laughed.

Chapter 14

Ceci awoke at 5:30 and couldn't believe how rested she was and couldn't imagine why. She must have had a fitful sleep as the blankets were on the floor and her pillow was wet from her perspiration. She never slept well. She couldn't ask Tim because he had been sleeping on the couch the last couple of nights.

She wondered what she was supposed to do that day. First, she needed to see what day it was. That was like telling a kid who asked how to spell a word, "Look it up."

"I don't know how to spell it. How can I look it up?" Very valid point, she would think.

How could she look to see what day or date it was if she didn't remember what month it was? She looked at the calendar and noticed that some months showed days with her notes written across them. On the tenth was scrawled "Damn!" in red and in smaller letters "fac. mtg." She didn't know if she had attended that meeting yet.

She couldn't ask any of the three what day it was because they would think she was nuts. She was so much sharper than any of them, with the slight exception of Jimmy catching up on the intelligence ladder. She would have to conjure up the right question so they wouldn't suspect anything might be wrong with her.

She went into the living room to wake up Tim. It was 5:40 and she figured he would be okay with being awakened. Just as she was about to tap him, she noticed his eyes were open as if he were waiting for her. He turned toward her and smiled. It wasn't a good-morning-my-sexy-love-and-how-are-you-this-morning greeting. She could have sworn it was a good-morning-my-damaged-baby greeting.

What do you need to know, his eyes asked her. It certainly came in handy that she was so much more alert than he was in just about everything in their lives. It wasn't always like that; no it wasn't. Tim had changed. He seemed very needy to her and he was quiet all the time.

If she didn't know better, she'd think the kids had changed, too. But that was understandable; they were growing up. Jimmy was the sensitive one; Jaime, the snip. Everyone had a role in the family. As a matter of fact, they were all needy—all except Ceci. She was the stoic one; she was the strong one; she was the glue that held the family together. Good thing for all of them that she was the stable one.

"Okay, Tim. Let's see if you can pass the test I am going to give my students today. Want to try?"

"Sure," he smiled. "Shoot."

"Let's see. Here's a toughie. What is today's date?"

With tears moistening his eyes, he said, "Let's go into the kitchen and see if I can figure it out."

"Ha ha," just as dumb as my students she teased and went with him.

Pointing to the calendar date, he said, "It's the tenth. How'd I do, Teach?"

Very casually, she nodded and said in teacher talk, "Excellent Timothy. Excellent. Go back to your couch now."

"How about some coffee, Babe?" Tim asked.

Damn, she had a faculty meeting that day, but at least she knew what day it was. Of course, she knew. What did he think she was, crazy or something? She didn't know what was wrong with Tim and she was getting worried. Every day seemed like a new hurdle.

Whatever damn day it was.

Chapter 15

Ceci found it very difficult to be serious when a group of people were soberly discussing something. She and Margot decided to take a mental health day from school. She always told her students when she did. It was validation for the kids for all the times they took days off and brought in forged school notes telling the teacher to please excuse Johnny because he had a sore throat. Sometimes Suzie couldn't get to school because her alarm didn't go off and she missed the bus. Ceci wondered at the number of alarms that malfunctioned. It was like when people told bill collectors that the check got lost in the mail. How that must have bothered the US Postal Service with its proud slogan of getting the mail out no matter what. Ceci preferred Wooton Basset's line in the radio comedy, *Adventures in Odyssey* when he said the mailman motto is "Rain or shine, snow or sleet, we deliver your mail (but sunny days are optional…)"

Ceci and Margot had gone on a senior citizens bus trip to an art museum in Manhattan. These trips always started the same way. The bus driver bowed to each lady and helped her board the bus.

"Marg, how many people do you think fall *into* buses?" She thought about the Farmer Gray cartoons of the 50s and what material those buses were made of that when all the people got on the bus, it swelled up to look like a giant ball on balloon wheels.

The two friends got comfortable and the bus headed for the city. Baldur, the tall Scandinavian who organized all the trips, took the microphone and his stare demanded silence. Nobody disobeyed Baldur who was really Hagar the Horrible.

"Welcome, everybody. I see soom familiar faces. Ha, and do I see soom teachers who may be playing hooky?" he said. He disliked teachers. That these particular teachers were Ceci and Margot no doubt multiplied his dislike and most likely precipitated it.

He pretended to be joking. "Easy money. Easy money. Do they appreciate it? Nooo. Do they forget we pay the taxes and they work for us. I am their boss!"

"Horrors! Yust our luck," Ceci whispered. "The boss *knows* we're here. Told you we should have worn soom disguises."

Before he told the riders what a wonderful tour he had planned, he prefaced with some personal information. The seniors were always happy to be privy to Baldur's private life, while Ceci and Margot found him boorish to be around with his prejudiced attitude toward educators.

Baldur said a major portion of his house had been damaged due to a burner explosion. Choruses of ohs and tsk-tsks. Things were not totally bad, he said. He was renting a gorgeous home, paid for by his insurance company. Short applause, proud of his insurance company.

"Yust as I was starting to think that things would get better when my friend's wife called and said my goot friend Oskar had a mild heart attack." Chimes of tsk-tsks. Baldur continued the that's-the-good-news, that's-the-bad-news shtick. With each wavelike emotion where the busload of concerned, retired ladies oohed, aahed, tsk-tsked and mini-cheered, Ceci and Margot just looked at each other and both were successful at subduing any expression. They stared straight ahead.

Until it happened.

"I started to see soom light in the tunnel," he said. Margot squeezed Ceci's hand.

"My prostate tests came back normal," he continued, "and my friend came home." Cheers.

"Then Oskie was rushed back to the hospital." Oh nos from the ladies. Ceci and Margot dared not repeat *Oskie* even to themselves.

"He survived the heart attack." More cheers.

"He was doing very well…" and just when Ceci and Margot thought they had escaped, Baldur finished them off with, "He came home two days later …" Still more cheers. "And died."

They looked at each other and both uncontrollably burst into soundless laughter—the kind that is in delay mode. The kind you know will get you in a heap o' doo-doo when the sound blasted through the voice box. They both knew it was a matter of time. The laughing bomb exploded from each of them, one laughing harder as the shrapnel from the other flew out. The other laughing even louder knowing they each were trying not to laugh, knew that the bus of concerned ladies was staring at them, knew how hysterically funny the whole situation was and knew damn well they looked like fools.

Which made them laugh even more.

Chapter 16

The last thing Tim wanted to do was to expose Ceci. Whenever he discussed her personality with anyone, he felt he was betraying her. He couldn't think of it as trying to help her because she never needed any help. She was Ceci who helped everybody. She was infallible, brilliant, perfect.

Tim was exhausted and he needed a quick shower to open his eyes this morning. He hadn't slept in their bed lately with Ceci's moaning in her sleep. He would have been flattered if they had been having sex, an act whose curtain hadn't risen in thirteen months.

He was not even going to call in. The Center knew he needed to take an indefinite leave since he, too, was near retirement. Ceci needed watching and they were fine with the arrangement. He had checked with the other psychiatrists as to her proposed treatment when it was time. For now, he was on call.

He looked in the mirror steadily as he took off his shirt. Still had pretty decent abs. His were not six-pack, but you could tell there was a can or two there for which he was proud.

He didn't exercise too vigorously although he did make overtures to do so. He went to the gym religiously and did the cross trainer for twenty minutes and some machines for another twenty. To him, climbing up the two flights of stairs and deliberately parking further from the entrance justified not staying more than forty minutes. Actually, he was bored at the gym. He felt he looked just fine. He interpreted the extended glances of middle-aged women as a measurement of his more than acceptable physical appearance.

Ceci used to love the way he looked. He could tell she still approved—not because she told him he looked good, but because she *didn't* tell him he looked lousy. With Ceci, the omission of an insult was a compliment. That was the best she could do.

"Don't think those little love handles make you look fat," she'd say. "You never had them before, but I see a lot of guys with worse ones than those." For effect, he wished he could blush. Then he would say, "Why, thank you, ma'am. You are too sweet." But he didn't bother. Whom did he need to please? His wife was gone or least left now more times than she was here.

Ceci couldn't help looking at the slightly opened bathroom door.

"I'd better close the door," she said to no one. "It is ajar." She loved that adjective.

"See that thing that is opened a little?" she'd say to the class. "What is that?"

"A door," the kids would say.

"And, my pretties. It is ajar."

"That's not a jar," Paul would say so happy he had a chance to jump in.

"Why sure it is, Bubba."

"It's not a jar. It's a door."

The class would laugh at the same worn joke and someone would mimic a fog horn. She'd laugh with them and compliment them that they knew the lines very well.

"God forbid—oops, not politically correct to say that— you remember any of the sonnets we worked on, but that door being ajar you all remember."

"Which door?" they'd continue.

"That door over there."

"You mean the one that's a jar?"

"Whateverrrrrr," she'd say, smirking, eyes fixed on the ceiling, getting an extra giggle from the girls. Then she would walk over to the door and slam it shut and say, "Now it's a door that's *not* ajar!"

That's what she loved about her students. They knew her jokes, as silly as they could be. She, in turn, played along by allowing them to make fun of her. Everybody knew how to play the game.

Too bad she had such a hard time playing husband-and-wife-love-each-other and husband-and-wife-still-get-a-kick-out-of-each-other. The rules used to be simple. Husband looked good and wife told him at every chance she got and husband kept himself looking sexy for wife. That was a game, but it was a game whose rules were made by husband and wife, played well by them, changed occasionally to accelerate the mood and, of late, broke the rules and dashed them into jail with no Monopoly Get Out of Jail Free card. They had each passed Go and never seemed to return around the board. Neither one realized the other traveled the whole board because one was sidetracked still trying to find the Park Place and Boardwalk of her life.

She wondered if everybody played. There must have been a survey. She knew how to conduct surveys because she had run so many in school. All kids loved to take surveys and loved more to see the results. They weren't interested in the evaluation of the results; they just liked to see how they all fared.

Ceci thought about the Miss Rheingold contest and how much she loved it when she was a young teen in Brooklyn. She remembered Gilda pointing out the pretty girls and asking Ceci who she thought was the prettiest. Did it matter that it was to decide who would be in the ads for a beer commercial? The memories of her and Gilda picking out who they thought would win the contest carried to her life in the classroom.

"Let's have a survey."

"Yeah," the students would say, not caring what it was for. She wanted to show her students of 2010 what was considered fun more than a half century ago. She had to fight off administration because they said she was advocating drinking beer.

"They stopped making Rheingold beer in the 70s, for God's sake. I want the kids to write a reaction paper to this kind of advertisement and to the promotion of such a product." Reluctantly, the administration agreed as it would only be a few months until Ceci retired. She had no intention of having the kids write a paper about it. She just wanted to have fun and get an enjoyable discussion out of it. The Rheingold tiara was the Burger King crown Marshall left behind after his birthday bash. She Googled the contestants of the 1964 competition, the last one she remembered voting in. The students made fun of the hairdos and voted, while Ceci nostalgically voted with the young teens of the 60s.

Each of her classes engaged in the same activity, each promising not to tell anyone else.

"Then the kids next year will already know who the Miss Rheingold was in 1964." She realized how silly that was and laughed with the kids. They promised not to tell anyone and, of course, the kids all told for two reasons: they loved doing something that was not allowed and they didn't give a flying fig for the kids next year. Those kids next year shouldn't be doing something against the school law anyway, they said. It just wasn't right. They would all slowly nod in agreement, each not meaning a single word.

She knew why the administration was being exceptionally lenient and indulgent. In a short while Ceci would disappear.

Chapter 17

Jaime had a lithe figure most girls in her school envied. In spite of her small breasts, she was curvy. Her long legs showed slight muscles on the calves from athletic prowess. She wore her clothes tight and enjoyed the attention from both boys and girls. Ceci wasn't happy with Jaime's look.

"If you went to the gym and you ate better, you could improve your own appearance," Jaime would start. "Not that there is anything wrong with how you look. I think that's the reason you disapprove of me so much."

"I don't disapprove of you. You could tone it down a bit, that's all. You are not leaving anything for the boys to wonder about."

"Tone it down a bit? Would I be your daughter if I toned *anything* down a bit?"

"It's your life, kid," Ceci said. "Do what you want with it. I won't interfere."

Yeah, like you mean that, Jaime thought.

If Jaime toned down her thought, toned down her voice, toned down her breathing, would that have pleased Ceci? Jaime was going to ask her mother, but thought better of it.

Just like Ceci, Jaime liked to project a false image. Her hair was naturally blond and she made an effort to prove correct the stereotypical belief of blonds being dumb. But she really didn't know any blonds who were any dumber than anyone else. Jaime knew a 57-year-old dumb, curly-headed brunette who had two kids, taught English at Alcmene High and thought the world was her yoyo, breaking the string for fun.

Too bad Jaime couldn't pick a mother. Do mothers pick daughters? She could always hang on to the hope that she was adopted and nobody told her. Then she could go searching for her biological mother. She rejected the idea fearing she would wind up with a mother more neurotic than the one she already had.

All of Jaime's friends were seeking out colleges. She knew she had to do the same, but she didn't want to. She decided she would be the antithesis of her mother and come out a better person, more successful, more loving and certainly more sane. She would not go to college, but somehow would manage to be independent and successful. That might prove to be difficult since she did not have any particular talents. She would work at any job to pay enough for her to get her own apartment and then she would concentrate on becoming successful.

Jaime liked challenges and becoming a success with no talent, no money, no education—well, that was going to take some doing.

For now, she had to talk some sense into her omniscient, successful mother. She knew Ceci would step to the podium and in her best teacher-talk attitude clear her throat and begin the speech she always seemed to have somewhere stuffed up in her sleeve. Ceci, the card trick magician, would extend her left hand and snake it up her right sleeve and walk her index and thumb up, crab-like, until the tips of her fingers felt the scroll-type rolled edge. Carefully, carefully she would snap her fingers onto a good size of the edge and pull, pull out down along her arm and unscroll the over-used, out-of-date speech.

"Money doesn't grow on trees... Someday when you get older... Youth is wasted on the young... When you get to be my age... Life is hard... If you tried... Your father and I..." The last undervalued, meaningless phrase is the one that always rankled Jaime. Her father and Ceci... As if Tim had any influence on whatever Ceci was pontificating. Ceci neither agreed with Tim, nor considered, any of his contributions to the family dynamic.

Jaime adored Tim.

"Your father can do no wrong..." Ceci would say as easily and as thoughtlessly as whenever someone sneezed. She really didn't care if God blessed sneezers. Sometimes Ceci was correct. Tim was always right in Jaime's eyes. Okay, okay. He got married. But Tim was young and he shouldn't have to pay for that mistake every day of his daughter's life.

"You don't even like him anymore. Why don't you just get a divorce?" Jaime said.

"Good Catholics do not divorce."

"Yeah, but you are not good Catholics."

"As opposed to you," Ceci said.

"Maybe if there was a God…"

"I will just chalk that up to your being young and stupid," Ceci said.

"Maybe so, Mrs. McKinney, but you gotta admit—there is no God in this damned house."

Chapter 18

Jimmy had just turned 15 and he liked the female interest he got for his height. He had always heard that boys spurt up at age 16 and he looked forward to those few more inches. 6'4" would be a nice height—tall enough to look down at just about everybody and not so tall as to be awkward and unappealing. His light brown lashes sweeping over hazel eyes enhanced his handsome face. He already needed to shave twice a week, but he so wanted to have a heavy beard so he could intentionally not shave giving him the popular look of the day. He liked his buzzed haircut and long sideburns that he would wear as long as he could until Tim strongly suggested that he shave them off a bit. If Tim were busy with Ceci, Jimmy could get away with a shave and "forget" to shave the sideburns. When the sideburns looked as though they were shaped like mutton chops, off they were lopped.

"Come on. They look good," he said.

"On James Madison, maybe. Cut 'em off."

"James Madison. James McKinney. Semantics. Don't stress, Dad."

"Off. Today."

"Okay. You can use this strategy on me for practice," he said.

"And that means…?"

"Well, you "suggest" to Mom when you have an opinion. All she has to do is *look* at you too long and heels click in blind obedience."

"That isn't fair, Jim, to me or Mom."

"Do you two even *have* a relationship?" Jimmy was sorry as soon as he had said this.

When Tim disagreed with Ceci, he did give Ceci sideglances as if to check to see if she was going to slide off some glass magic carpet. Tim would watch it as it flew around the room, his hands always ready to either stop the carpet speed or slow it down. If he couldn't do either, he would be able to redirect it so that it would crash into a bed or soft down pillow and comforter. Then the glass wouldn't shatter and spray all over their lives.

"Jimmy, have you read much of Langston Hughes?"

"Wait, don't tell me, 'Life for me ain't been no crystal stair'. Hey, Dad, what do you think it has been for us?"

Sometimes Tim forgot how perceptive his children were.

"You are always picking up pieces. What kind of existence is that?" said Jimmy.

His son was right. Tim rode crystal shotgun for crystal marauders ready to hold up a crystal stage after climbing broken crystal stairs.

Jimmy thought of his grandfather Gino.

"You should be on a stage," Grandpa always said when Jimmy was showing a little too much bravado. "There's one leaving at five." It was so corny, but it was what Jimmy longed to hear right now. He knew he should stop and give his father some leeway.

He needed to hear any words from Gino. They didn't have to be brilliant words. Or was it his grandfather he longed to have back? Jimmy thought that when Gino Scarpelli was alive, he was the corniest guy around. Now Jimmy's vegetable-of-life diet was lacking the carbohydrate that was the tastiest—corn.

He believed in God and was determined that when he entered Heaven and met his grandpa, he would ask him to say nothing but nerdy things. Nerdy jokes. He was the master of the reason for the barump bumps.

He missed Grandpa. Gino died when Jimmy was nine and he never was able to do the same things with Tim. There was a special magic about grandpas. They were the untarnished heroes in life and if a kid was lucky enough to have one close by, that kid had better not be a jerk and let that goofy old guy slip past. There is no better fun than with a grandpa. Who else would answer any question no matter how inane the subject? All subjects were important to the grandfather if they were important to the grandson. Period. Grandpa always had the time for Jimmy.

Gino was a tall man and out of loyalty to him, Jimmy did not want to grow taller than he. Grandpa had thick wavy hair, and Jimmy hoped he would retain his tresses throughout his life. He liked when girls flirted, especially when the really older ones eyed him over. How many 14-year-olds had 18-year-old girls look at them as if they were box office Adonises? This impression became a certainty every time Jaime's friends came by and saw Jimmy.

"Him??" he could hear Jaime say. "He is so annoying. No, he's not cute. He's ugly as sin."

Chapter 19

Ceci decided to assign some quality thought to Tim. Didn't he know that he was wasting his time trying to save her? He could be helping others the way he was trained to. Then he could find a way to carve a path to Heaven. With this holy and blessed pave job, he could slide upward.

"I know. I know," she said looking up. "This is a bit gravity-challenging, but that's how it is when Heaven, God, angels and all those other supremes are involved." She did not want to get too distracted, so she exhaled and continued.

"Stay with me here, okay, Bigshot Creator? Tim would slide up to the Pearly Gates. I'd watch him in preparation for when I will eventually take the puffy celestial road and slide up, up, and bam! I'd crash against those locked gates. Who would be there to open them for me?"

She knew it would be her brother Alan.

She walked up the driveway and thought of reasons she liked autumn so much. The smell in the air told her that winter was approaching, that's true, but now it seemed like there was a perseverance to Nature. Everybody loved summer—except Ceci—and few people wanted it to end. She supposed if the

Earth goddess Demeter was in a bad mood, the goddess was neither afraid nor interested any longer in what her mortals wanted.

Ceci understood the goddess perfectly. Demeter was still peeved at her brother Hades for the stunt he pulled when he abducted her daughter—his niece—Persephone. The people on earth wanted summer to last longer. Ha, tough on them. They'd have to wait another year to feel the sun warming them and helping to make their paltry gardens blossom. If Ceci had a garden, she thought, it would probably be paltry.

Persephone was not only Demeter's daughter, but her heart, her self. She complained to her brother Zeus; she complained to other immortals and took out her sadness and anger on her Earthly charges. When Demeter took summer away, she teased to remind her children that not only was summer gone, but a wet, snowy and harsh time would follow—like it or not. And just in case they forgot that autumn followed summer, she added coolness tantalized with the aroma of orangey foliage.

Ceci liked the sound of crunching leaves underfoot along the brick driveway.

"Yes, Angelo—*Michel*angelo your mother should have named you—the money you charged for this job was well worth it. *Artigiano*, that's what you are." Actually, he was and her driveway was the envy of the best landscape driveway designers on Long Island. She especially liked that it had that old European stone bumpy feel. Car tires and strong springs absorbed most of the bumps. Treading on the surface with brown crusty leaves temporarily repaving it was comfortable and soothing to her.

Ceci was both killing and rebirthing the leaves. From the vantage point of the uninformed onlooker, it would seem that these brown leaves were now crushed, near-powdered dead pieces. Stupid, stupid people, she thought. These precious oak, sycamore and maple donations were not given recklessly. A higher order deemed they leave their mother. Because of Ceci, these leaves had an important mission; they allowed the next batch to grow. They would be born and show their strength in their greenness. They'd stay long enough to fool the observer into trusting that the world was stable.

Then they, too, would decide to give up the life they had and let some of their greenness depart. They would let the autumnal-hued deadness—so pleasant to the onlooker—fall, but stagger their departures. What cleverness, Ceci thought, one day green and the next burnt-orange, charred-yellow and ruby-red. Looking up, she said,

"I would do the same thing."

Today, though, these fallen foliage had to be unceremoniously raked up and discarded.

"What a travesty," she said. She thought of the leaf-raking her landscapers would do very soon.

"Do you enjoy being swirled around and brushed against each other until you are piled up?" She felt a little sad that the rake cycle would be sacrificed to a store-bought, man-made leaf blower. How heartless a demise, she thought. Sucked up or blown to kingdom come. Then what? Mulched?

"How utterly barbaric," she said to her driveway. "And you just let it all happen."

She stood for a moment and addressed the leaves, "Not today, ladies and gentlemen. Today I will validate your existence and transform you into delicate tiny mosaic beauties." She pressed them into the dirt preserving them until the winter when they would be covered by their natural hoary blanket.

Ceci climbed the three brick steps and entered the foyer, not caring that it was quite a difference in temperature from when she was home all day. She kept the thermostat at 68 and preferred the cold. Tim always gave in to the whining of the kids and raised the temperature to suit their needs. It was so typical of Tim. After a day of teaching teenagers, most educators liked to come home to a quiet house. Lately, her house automatically got quiet when she entered and today it was even quieter.

Tim was sitting in the living room with the lights off. She wanted to make a joke about his lights being out, but she didn't. She always made sure she confused his being a kind man with being a fool.

She cautiously walked to where he probably was sitting, on the recliner, but not reclining. She didn't even check to see if he were breathing. She stopped doing that to Tim. Tim would always be breathing.

"You okay?" she asked, more out of duty than interest.

"Yeah. I'm good," he said as he put on the light and got up to kiss her.

"No," she said. "You don't have to. You look tired."

"I am tired. Very."

Ceci did not like that tone and before it made her uncomfortable, she shrugged it off. That was typical Tim, she thought—nuts, moody and going off the deep end. He could really use some help. "Something smells good."

"I'll get dinner on the table," he said.

"No, really. Something smells good. Is it you?"

He looked at her and wondered if she were being the usual wise-ass. She looked serious so Tim answered seriously.

"I put on some of Jimmy's cologne."

"Ha, ha. Are you sure it wasn't Jaime's?"

"You never stop, do you?" Tim said and went into the kitchen.

She knew she should apologize assuring him she was an ass, but she didn't.

Even though she was.

Chapter 20

When Ceci needed to laugh, she would think of crazy things that happened in school. They weren't crazy things by her standards, but they made the kids laugh like loons. She would have, too, if she remembered how.

Steven Temple had been driving her and all the rest of the faculty up the Alcmene High School wall. What was worse was that this year Ceci had been triple-whammied by her schedule. He was in her homeroom for 27 minutes; with her in her lunch period duty for another 42 minutes and in her English class immediately following for 42 more minutes. 111 minutes a day with Steven Temple entitled one to a free pass to the heaven of one's choice.

A disappointment and embarrassment to Judge William J. Temple, president of the school board, Steven was the reason Alcmene High formed their Alternate School program. The Alternate School, also known by the students as the Flight Deck, was supposed to be a rehabilitative school environment. Originally an empty storage suite above the cafeteria, the only way the kids could enter the Alternate School was from the back entrance near the teachers' parking lot. Heaven forbid they came in contact with the "adjusted and academically superior" varsity of this South Shore school.

"Alternate to what?" she'd say, "Jail? The loony bin?" Because of his incorrigible behavior, Steven was one of the first in line of many students who much needed, but didn't get, an education. The only one who benefited from the Alcmene Alternate School when it opened its doors the first year was the teacher, physical education coach Kenny Richards. No one who taught in the content areas or in the electives wanted to teach there. They felt there were less painful ways to commit suicide.

The Alternate School was perfect for Coach Kenny Richards. He had a need and this faux school/pre-prison environment was ideal for him. His marriage was disintegrating. There were no salvageable pieces from which to work if either he or his wife wanted to, which neither did. Kenny was one year from retirement and had neither patience nor inclination to talk school shop with the vintage teachers, let alone the newbies. So this converted four-room cafeteria supply area was ideal.

Kenny's office was equipped with sink, refrigerator, microwave, couch, computer, phone, and bathroom. The students had a bathroom in the tiny hall, a mini lunch room for bagged lunches, all paid for by the town residents grateful these kids would never mingle with their own kids in the regular school setting just one flight down. The Alternate School's classroom was well stocked with five books for each of the major subjects, none of which Kenny was certified to teach. But these five kids were not meant to succeed academically. In reality, it was an environment which merely postponed most of their criminal activities until they were legally able to drop out of school. And they all did, having learned very little from Kenny except that he didn't hate them the way all the other teachers did. Kenny didn't care about them either way. As long as they didn't misbehave, they could do as much or as little school work as they wanted. They all received Ds and everybody was happy.

It would take twenty years and many crimes for the administration to make the Alternate School a real place of rehabilitation and learning—for the student, that is, and not just for the teacher.

On an exceptionally stressful day, one of Steven Temple's regular classroom teachers was trying to put up a bulletin board before the end of the period. She assigned busy work for the class so she could get the board done. After repeated questions of "What can I do? What can I do?" from Steven, the teacher said,

"Do anything you want!"

Steven was sent to the dean for the second time that week.

"Standing on top of a teacher's desk, pretending to masturbate over the attendance book will not be tolerated, young man. It is not in the Alcmene High School Code of Conduct," said the dean.

"Oh no? Geez, coulda sworn I saw that in one of the paragraphs. Oops, my bad," said Steven as he now attempted to climb atop the dean's desk.

After a meeting with Superintendent Abramson, a few teachers and Steven's father, it was agreed that a week of out-of-school suspension and weekly visits to the school psychiatrist were in order. Ceci had suggested a firing squad, but they didn't listen to her. Perhaps if the week before he hadn't Crazy-glued Ceci's desk calendar to her desktop, her suggested punishment might have been lighter.

"Then how about a little caning?" she added.

The reason the suspension wasn't longer was that no one volunteered to homeschool Steven.

Ceci had been frustrated and furious with Steven Temple's shenanigans, his meanness, his... Stevenness. This day at lunch was the proverbial straw that broke the camel's back for Ceci. He had spread ketchup on the chair of a chubby, gentle-natured girl and laughed like a hyena as she cried in mortification when he said,

"*Some*body has to stop buying Kotex Light Days pads. Better go for the bigger ones, girl. By the looks of your butt, the super-humongous ones might not even be enough." As she ran out of the cafeteria, he yelled, "hey, when you sit on a piano, does it disappear?"

The dean was out of his office, so the secretary sent Steven on to his next class—Ceci's. After all, the secretary thought, it was the dean's job to deal with kids like Steven.

And anyway, Mrs. McKinney could handle Steven. She was the master in total control.

Ceci walked into her classroom and the rowdy bunch led by Steven seemed to dare her to teach. She sat in the wheeled metal arm chair that she had taken from the math chairperson's office. The chair was a bit rickety, but it rolled. What else did one need from a teacher's chair? Arms and wheels. At least a bit of comfort was afforded her every day. She sat in the chair and tried to enjoy its whooshing as it depressed when she sat.

Steven was seated as far from Ceci as possible. A little further away and he would be in the courtyard—which was always a temptation for Ceci, the winter months being the most desirable. The back seating, however, was to his advantage. He already had the kids riled up from lunch and it was getting very noisy in class. She told them to be quiet and, of course, they needed to be admonished more than once.

Still seated, she briskly walked the chair in time with her flaring temper, and the wheels caught on a stapler a student had dropped earlier. She could feel the chair starting to tip as she was chastising Der Steven Monster. She waited for the inevitable. The clanking, thudding and swooshing of chair/butt/clothes meeting the floor prompted total silence from the class. She only had three or four seconds to react the right way.

They were quiet and stared at her as she got to her knees, hands on the floor and pushed herself upright. She looked at the gawking students and forced herself to laugh. She did not think it was funny and her body did not feel like it was funny. She was so angry with Steven that she normally wouldn't even *consider* the possibility of a scintilla of humor. She had no choice and started to bluff a laugh—thank goodness for the acting ability of teachers—and she succeeded. When the class saw her laughing at what they thought was the funniest thing their nubile minds ever experienced, the room thundered and whooped in delight. She kept the pasted smile in place as she joined in, trying to keep her clenched teeth from showing. She waited for the class to settle down and finished her grammar lesson. As the students were leaving for their next class, Ceci reminded them of what a jerk she must have looked like.

She dreaded going to the cafeteria the next day. She didn't think she could handle being ridiculed. Nobody said anything to her; nobody referenced the day before. Steven had told so many people the rest of that day that both he and his audience were tired of hearing him talk about what a klutz Mrs. McKinney was.

She was the master in total control. She decided not to think this too long.

Chapter 21

It was a lot of effort to keep up the appearance of taking total command in a chaotic atmosphere. Ceci usually was the catalyst in the chaos and she used to love it. It was her way of surviving. That's what was happening to her now every day. She was surviving.

More than reading Sylvia Plath's work, she loved reading *about* Sylvia Plath. She associated with Plath and sometimes she wished she had the guts to kill herself as the author did. She read and re-read Plath's *The Bell Jar*. My whole life is a bell jar, she thought. She wasn't sure if hers paralleled Plath's exactly, though.

Ceci created her own filled bell jar. Each portion of disappointment and anger was mixed with the solvent of laughter. Was the laughter now so thinned out that it transformed into liquefied sorrow and disappointment? Would it ever be possible for the mixture to thicken and if so, what would be the ingredient needed and what would be the formula? Only when she could figure out which was which could she make any real determination of what direction her life would take. Right now, she was in some control. She just could not reconcile that Tim couldn't understand that and go along with everything. Why couldn't *he* be the solvent and her emotions and actions the firmer components?

"Yep. A bell jar," she said.

There were so many tiny furies Ceci mentally contained, and she made sure they didn't emerge to the forefront of her psyche. If they did show their faces, then she would either be forced to deal with them or just let them languish somewhere just beneath the surface. Languishing emotions ultimately congealed into something else, the form not known to her although owned by her. *What is the meaning of life. Why is there air?*

"Sounds like something from a Bill Cosby routine," she said. She laughed at her own answer, "to fill up basketballs and volleyballs, stupid."

"Who made us?" Sister Mary Grace quizzed.

"God made us," 6-year-old Cecilia Scarpelli answered.

"Why did God make us?"

"He made us to …"

Wow, God gets credit for lot, Ceci realized. He was, at times, also a major screw up. At least with her life, He was. Funny how Ceci blamed Him for the lousy stuff and when things got good, she took the credit.

"What a lousy master planner You are," Ceci said. "Tough job being the boss, eh?" She thought of a line from Woody Allen's *Love and Death* when he said, "if it turns out that there is a God, I don't think that He's evil. I think that the worst you can say about Him is that basically He's an underachiever."

Ceci knew that Jesus must have had a great sense of humor. How often must He have held up his hands and said,

"Hey, somebody's got to do it." The quintessential underachiever.

"Damn," she said. "Where is a science teacher when you need him?" She should have taken a dual major: English and Science. Then she would have all he answers. She started to sing,

"Oh, what a lov-elly bunch of psycho-nuts."

She was getting so tired of her role of entertainer, mother, wife, problem-solver, creative genius, chairperson, underling, lackey, superior force. Who made her the superior force, by the way? She did, of course. She had to because people needed her.

Whom did she need? Whom did she have when she swung herself around, arms extended to feel for something tangible upon which to hook and shake herself free from the sticky things that were making her itch—for something, for some place simple and quiet.

"Wouldn't it be nice," Ceci said, "to live where nobody could talk, or hear or even run anywhere so that there would be guaranteed stillness. Well, maybe the use of one hand to write might be allowed."

Chapter 22

Ceci didn't know why she got these feelings. For no apparent reason, her body, her mind and her emotions would feel a kind of calm. It was warm liquid slowly drizzling over her. Not too much, not too little. Like the porridge. Maybe it was porridge escaping from her childhood. She didn't know what porridge was when she was a child, but knew that in Brooklyn, amid dilapidated row houses, in a railroad flat with just the living room to sleep in, she knew porridge must be good.

Ceci didn't like when she felt happy and didn't know why. She didn't trust it, so she had to suppress it and lock this soft, velvety, warm stranger, happiness, in the cold jail of her heart behind gory bars and rusted lock tumblers. She only used this stranger to absorb the weeping wounds within her bloodied heart so that it could sop them up and make the chambers a bit drier to be able to house more. She stopped herself from even wanting to like this stranger. What would happen if it figured out what Ceci was really like and then turned on her and destroyed her totally? She looked forward to Thursdays to be with her yearbook club. These meetings were more than just the kids working on the pages for the Alcmene Yearbook. She was pretty sure she could get away with continuing to conduct the group session format which immediately followed the regular meetings.

She had been doing this for years and each year the kids loved them. And each year she seemed to shift from moderator to participating member. This year she was unable to be anything but member and a needy member at that.

Oh boy, have I got a few things to say, she thought.

She didn't know if she ever did divulge her feelings to this group. She really hoped she did. Lately she didn't remember much and it seemed to get harder to focus.

Chapter 23

Jaime stood staring at the inside of the refrigerator. "Mom, there's nothing in the friggin' fridge. Where is Dad, anyway?"

Funny how Jaime presumed that Tim did all the cooking and motherly stuff.

"Can you not say 'friggin'. It is so, so low-class."

"Then, where is the exact location of Father, o perfect maternal relative?" Jaime could be quite nasty.

"Don't know. Is it his night out with the boys? Hmm," she said as she nudged Jaime out of the way of the refrigerator/TV set. "I don't know what he left for the family to eat. Only thinks of himself, that guy."

Jaime moved away from the refrigerator and let the door she had been keeping open with her left arm swing into her mother.

"Oops," she said. "I was just thinking of myself, I guess."

"What makes you so mean?" Ceci said, but really didn't want to know. "Call Dominoes. Your father left a coupon somewhere for $3 off."

"Oh, okay, Mommy. Now we can eat a nice warm meal."

"Jaime!" Jimmy yelled from his room. "Easy."

"Sir James of the Shield of Cecilia has spoken. The revolution of the sun has begun."

"The Earth," he corrected

"The revolution of the friggin' *Earth* will be affected, Mother," she said turning to Ceci who was dialing the pizzeria and asking for delivery, "and for our repast," Jaime continued, "let us gather round the table holding hands and break pizza together."

Tim got home at 1 am and didn't even try to walk quietly. It didn't matter; he knew Ceci pretended she was asleep. It made it easier on him that way. He set the alarm for 6 am and didn't worry if it disturbed Ceci because she was usually lying with her eyes open, anyway. He didn't know when she slept or if she did sleep. Physiologically, she had to, but he never knew when. When she was in bed in sight of him, her eyes were always closed. Was she trying to fall asleep? He didn't think she was.

Tomorrow was Thursday and he was expecting her to come home from school a little stranger than normal. He was bracing up for anything. Being with his old Brooklyn friends helped, but definitely did not substitute for his own needs which were not as great as they were when he first got married. He knew she was quirky and hot-tempered, but that's what he had liked about her. Now those traits were tramping on dangerous mental ground. The husband in him prayed these traits wouldn't develop further into something physical; the clinician in him knew prayer was not enough. Approaching his wife with the suggestion she needed psychiatric help, to Ceci, would have been tantamount to abandoning her, murdering her. He had to wait for more signs. And the signs were there and getting easier to recognize.

All of his fears about Ceci were surfacing and Tim didn't know if he could treat them. The Messine Center for Mental Health felt he could. He had been working for them since he got his Ph.D. more than thirty years ago and he welcomed their proposal. Ease out of his career while treating his wife.

"Simple for them to say. They don't know Ceci." Actually, most of his colleagues did know her and did commiserate with this monumental task.

The alarm rang and up she was. Into the bathroom, shower turned on. Thirty minutes later, she was transformed into a teacher, face powdered and lipsticked, blazer buttoned, briefcase in hand. Where was her green bag? She liked that she had twelve different colored leather handbags. She prided herself on how svelte and color-coordinated she always was. Not that anyone noticed at home.

It only took her fifteen minutes to get to school and by 7:15 she had plenty of time for the 7:25 sign in. Nothing unusual today. It was just a typical day when teenagers defied anyone to teach them something.

And Ceci did. And she did it well.

"Donna, bring the proofs here, will you?" A yearbook deadline was two weeks away and Ceci liked a no-pressure deadline meeting. The yearbook was coming along very nicely and she would be entering retirement having left a beautiful, professional Alcmene yearbook, *The Cardinal,* her last gift to the students.

The yearbook meeting was over and her editors put everything away. They rearranged the desks and put them in a circle. Donna would be presiding.

"You sitting in the middle, Mrs. McKinney?"

"No, today, I am going to be one of you. Today I will be a disturbed person asking for help." The group accepting her ribbing.

Donna looked at the clock. "4:45. Great. We have more than an hour. Everybody okay with that?"

The rest of the group assayed and adjusted themselves in their seats for a good ride.

Ceci exhaled louder than she needed to.

"You want to go first, Mrs. McKinney?"

"No." She would act coy for awhile. Donna looked at George. "How goes it?"

"Everybody *knows,*" he began. He got up and sashayed to the window unable to control his effeminate walk.

"So? What's the problem?" said Donna.

"Don't know if I can do it," said George.

"Do what, for heaven's sake? It is done. You are a cooked goose and ready to be served," Ceci interrupted and the group cat-called.

"Has anybody said anything to you? If they do, I'll make them an offer they can't refuse," Kyle teased in a Don Corleone accent.

"So, then you think it would be okay if I came in dressed in my mom's clothes wearing her red spikes?"

"No, no, Georgie Boy" said Kyle. "Last time you drilled a hole in my instep and I couldn't walk for a week." George pretended to be angry and punched Kyle. They all laughed and moved on. Donna looked past Ceci to Marc.

"Marc? How's it going?"

The group session lasted a little past six and the parents would be parked outside the school annoyed that this teacher worked their kids too damn hard and had no conception of time or consideration for people who *really* worked. It was dinnertime and they couldn't be waiting outside the school forever.

The students said their good nights to each other and Ceci waited until they were all with their parents.

Then she sashayed to her car.

Chapter 24

Ceci couldn't believe how fast the week went by. So dull. So unCeci-ish. It seemed that she didn't mind so much her life rushing past as long as it stopped and waited for those after-yearbook meeting sessions.

The Alcmene yearbook club meetings had become very popular. Students who joined the club were not as much interested in creating a yearbook as they were to be involved in group talk and personal analysis. Ceci wondered how administration would look upon these unauthorized sessions, unsanctioned by the Guidance Department whose main mission was to work with troubled kids.

"Those counselors walk around with spray cans of anti-depressants. I swear, they look forward to teen tragedies so they can play psychiatrist. My meetings are harmless, but helpful as well," she told Margot one time.

"You sure you know what you're doing," Margot said. "I mean with Tim being a shrink and all?"

"Him?? He lives in a world different from the rest of us. I'm telling you, Marg, he has lost touch. Really." She paused for a moment and added sardonically, "Why, I don't think he could recognize a psycho case if he slept with her."

She never asked for permission to run these groups. The kids and their parents never complained and she really didn't care now about Board of Education repercussions because she was retiring in a few short months. She enjoyed her role and she was personally getting a lot out of the meetings.

"Michelle," moderator Donna said, "you go first."

"I can't stand how my mom constantly belittles my dad," said Michelle.

"Your dad is a big boy," Donna said. "Why can't he take care of himself? You're just the kid in the family equation."

"Who do you think is wrong, Michelle? Does your dad ask to be mistreated?" Ceci asked.

"How could anybody ask to be mistreated? Really, Mrs. McKinney. You *are* reaching a little, aren't you?"

"No need to get testy, Michelle ma belle."

"That's what we're here for," said Donna. "Pesty and testy. We learned from the besty, right Mrs. M?" And the group chuckled more out of politeness than for considering the talk humorous. There were no airy problems within this group.

"Okay, so run it by us again, Michelle," Ceci began. "Why does your dad suck?"

The group whistled.

"Well, all of youse talk like that. Why can't I? Seriously." Ceci liked the way she was able to toggle the conversation focus. The kids were very capable of keeping up with her. She wondered if group toggle was like group hug. Well, they did that too, kind of.

"You know, my cherubs, you don't have to hug somebody to hug somebody the way you don't have to stab somebody to stab somebody. People can bleed without blood, cry without tears, suffer without wounds. Do wounds fester for no reason? Do people hurt for no reason? " Ceci said.

Frustrated at not seeing their faces illuminant with understanding, she sang again in her best cockney,

"Oh, what a lov-elly bunch of psycho-nuts. There they are a-standing in a row-ow…" She looked around and thought they either didn't know the coconut song or they were just not getting it today.

"Am I the only one who is sportin' a brain? Well, I'm having fun, anyway. Too bad you all decided not to attend the meeting. Okay, time to go. I'm done. And thank God, it's six o'clock. I'm sure all the mama chickens are waiting for their precious hatchlings. No, wait, you're not even there, yet. You're more like eggs. Better go—fast, else you will be addled and scrambled and done once over light."

The students filed out, the boys high-fiving each other and the girls air cheek kissing.

Michael had particularly bothered her at group tonight. His stuttering seemed to annoy her totally. She thought he was being more affective than he had to with his inability at times to get the first word of a sentence out. She had him in eighth period English. Surely, it took more than one more period to produce a stutter like he had today. What did he sound like in homeroom? Clear, casual? In a nine-period day, eighth period was just like the last of the day. He couldn't have developed this in a few hours. And every day? Why on earth, she wondered, didn't the other kids notice it?

She understood he had a precondition to stammering, but she could swear that sometimes he stammered more than other times. Sometimes the stuttering got worse. She wished he would come in with a more controlled attitude. She would have to look a little closer next time. If she had to demand he stop talking, then so be it. Ceci ran the world; let no one forget it.

Her empty classroom transformed into a morgue, eerily quiet, and she liked it that way. She could hear the distant push of a janitor's broom passing over the day's dirt. She could make out how many gum wrappers were on the floor by the mild break in the gentle, even swoosh sound. She could make out the cleaner straight indent the wrapper made through the thin layer of dust that still managed to remain on the floor. It was barely discernible; in fact it was not noticeable at all, but Ceci knew it was there. She could hear it. It was almost like the broom had a faint stutter to the even language of the sweeping motion. Ceci imagined Marshall's life to be like her room.

And she wanted that life.

Chapter 25

This time Ceci drove up the driveway, the front bumper of her car butting the garage door. She didn't feel like walking on any leaves. She didn't feel like blending with nature. She had done all the blending during the yearbook meeting that she cared to. She knew she should have let the kids speak more, but they were not cooperating. They seemed satisfied with the progression. Was she the only one who had clarity? Lately, it was the same everywhere she went.

That Michael hogged the whole meeting with his damned stuttering, she thought.

"When an audience is engrossed with you, no matter how you speak," she would tell her students before they gave an oral report in class, "you won."

Michael won. She didn't like him today. How could she be his hero if she couldn't help him? Maybe she just needed to see what his world was like. There was the rub.

She entered the living room and suddenly felt a draining sensation from her shoulders down her arms to her fingertips. No pain, just a draining like a one-way transfusion.

She stood there and exhaled deeply. Tim, busy in the kitchen, heard her enter and he peeked in.

"Babe?"

"Uh?"

"You okay?"

"My love," she said in a Dracula voice, "I feel a little drained."

"Okay, Bela," she thought she heard him say, but he probably didn't.

"Try Frank Langella. He was a cuter Dracula," she said and didn't know if he had heard her. "Nobody associates Dracula with Bela Lugosi anymore."

He wiped his hands on his apron and walked quickly to her. She guessed she had been speaking now loud enough for Jaime to hear.

"Mom?"

"It is I, child," said Ceci. "Why isn't Jimmy vaulting down the stairs to ask if I am home?" She began hanging up her coat and said, "Should I make it seem like home if I toss it onto the couch? Then at least we'd know Jaime was home."

She decided to fling her coat, missed, its sleeves caught in the cushion and the rest hanging over.

"Oh, look Timmy, Ceci's stuck in the couch. Bad Ceci," she said and smacked the coat.

Jaime stared at her mother and controlled any typical Jaime response. Ceci was kind of disappointed because she was in the mood and welcomed a little confrontation with her smart aleck daughter. Whom did she take after, she wanted to know.

Something smelled good, but she decided not to tell Tim. She thought long and hard, reconsidered and called to him,

"Wha...wha...t are you cook...cooking?"

Tim came closer. He looked up through the slightly spiraled staircase and motioned to Jimmy to stay upstairs. He gave an out-of-character stern look and Jimmy stayed put.

Tim made sure Jaime hadn't decided to accept Ceci's call out for a verbal three rounds. Jaime could spar well and sometimes, more lately it seemed, Tim was in Jaime's corner sponging her and giving her pep talks. These talks were non verbal, but very loud to Ceci. She didn't care, though. She didn't have a corner because she didn't need help.

"Don't look so...so...so...dumb. Wha...w...w...what are you cooking? S...s....s....mells good."

Tim decided to sleep in the bed tonight with Ceci. He stroked her face, especially her lips as she said,

"D...do I have f...food on my l...l...lips?"

"No, love," he said and thought he saw a tear form, but he was wrong.

His tear had dropped onto her eye.

Chapter 26

It was Thursday and she thought about canceling both the yearbook meeting and the group session afterward.

"Damn," she remembered, "I've got to check these galleys." Ceci was satisfied with the work the kids had done. The pictures were scaled properly where no one had a tall thin body and no one had those wide squishy faces you see in the carnival funhouse mirrors. By the end of ninth period, all the students started to look like that to Ceci. The windows looked stretchy and wavy. The clock looked like a Salvador Dali painting.

Actually, she liked Dali's work—not his life, but his rubbery paintings. Her favorite was the popular surreal, "The Persistence of Memory." One reason was that Tim had bought her a print of it the third week they were dating. She had admired it when they visited one of the art museums in Manhattan. Another reason was that it was her life: melting and oozing away.

She decided against canceling the club meeting. Desks were dragged into the middle of the room, the fourteen making a functioning circle. She wanted to sit in the middle this time.

The students surmised why. There was the usual recapping of what had taken place at the last session. She sat and exaggeratedly exhaled. She stared at each student until someone, either out of discomfort or boredom of the silence, spoke up. It was Donna.

"How goes it Mrs. McKinney?"

"None of your business, really," Ceci started. No one spoke and Ceci could hear her own voice somewhere from the next room, next town, next world. She heard it and wondered why she had left the room.

"Stick those tissues where the sun don't shine, girl," she continued, out of character for their Mrs. McKinney. Ceci usually said silly and benign phrases to keep the kids on track and to remove any possible nervousness even though they were a tough, emotionally-hardened group. She foot dragged and wheeled her chair until she slid herself in the only available slot among the circle. With her blazer sleeve, she wiped her clean desk as if she were trying to clear her mind. Satisfied, she folded her hands and smiled at the group.

Today would belong to Bernadette Berman. She coughed her usual cough. There was no need for Ceci to suggest Bernadette go to a doctor since she went to the doctor, every kind of doctor, on a regular basis. She coughed. She scratched. She adjusted her neck. Bernadette was constant motion, but the coughing was all anybody ever associated with her. It seemed like she never said more than a sentence without a cough to complete it or begin the next. After a while, people got used to it.

"I have decided to tell my mom," Bernadette said.

"Well, hear, hear. Want an audience on which to practice?"

"No, thanks Mrs. McKinney. I have practiced telling her about my father so often that I say it in my sleep."

"The sandman must find yours quite the tedious assignment. He probably quietly steals past your bed hoping you don't notice."

"Unlike what her father does," Kyle said. The group whooped at Kyle and Bernadette laughed along with them. Laughing was the catalyst. Bernadette trusted this group of friends and looked forward to the sessions.

She was coughing more than normal. Kyle got up and from behind put his arms around Bernadette.

"Ya know how hard this is," he said, "not to go and blow his brains out?"

Bernadette turned her head and smiled at him and touched his hands. She got up and walked to the exit. Ceci caught up with her.

"Better find the right time to tell your mom. I can't wait another day. It's tomorrow, or I go to the police," Ceci said.

"Mrs. McKinney! You promised me you'd let me tell her in my own time."

"Well, Bernadette, your time is my time and time's up."

Bernadette would be home in a half hour and she was going to approach her mother when they were alone. She would have to endure her father's touching on the ride home, but she knew it would only last for a few minutes. Not enough time for her to cry like when she was in her bed and her father tried to muffle the cries with his groin.

Chapter 27

Ceci was not able to stop thinking of Bernadette.

"Tomorrow that low-life of a father will never be near another child again. His demise will be Bernadette's rebirth. Damn him," she said as she had been saying for more than two weeks to herself. She wondered if she would remember to report him. What a shame it would be, she thought, if she forgot.

She drove home and stayed in her driveway for a few minutes.

"Got to get things settled a bit," she said and checked the mirror to see if she was in order. She forced herself to be in a good mood. Nearing the front door, she stopped, stared at it for a few seconds and entered.

She had 120 compositions to grade and wanted to use her new red gel pen. She liked the fat pens that just clicked and voila, out gelled the crimson determiner of whether the student was grounded or rewarded for the day or even the week. She felt unusually generous when she graded this time and surmised that there would be a week of going out, watching TV or listening to iPods for most of her students.

"Hello. Hello. Hello. Da mudder is home."

"Hey, Mom," Jimmy yelled.

"Babe," acknowledged Tim. Jaime didn't bother, but Ceci still heard, "Very big deal. She's home."

"A glass of the finest amontillado would be great, Fortunato," she said.

"I'd say Poe be damned, but he probably was," Tim mumbled. Tim poured her a glass of sangria, and she gulped it. He never liked when she did that because it would make her light-headed in minutes. Now after her behavior these past few months, she needed to be mellow to be dealt with, to be tolerated. She motioned for more and Tim willingly poured a second.

"Got any peaches?"

"Sorry, Love," Tim said.

"Who cares? I will live on the edge and drink it straight." She finished her second glass and asked Tim for a refill.

"Hold on, that will make three. You won't be able to see your gradebook, let alone the rows and columns.

"Oh stop being such an old poop. Be a pal," she said in a voice which sounded so pleasing to Tim that deep down he didn't care if she guzzled the whole bottle.

He poured and urged her to sit with him on the couch. She acquiesced and leaned her head onto his shoulder as they walked, making them look like a caring man helping a drunk lady which was quite the accurate portrayal of this happy sober man.

"How was school today?"

"I pulled off another I-know-who-you-are-even-though-I-don't."

Tim knew he was about to be entertained. He loved when she related stories from school. These were better than some of the untold tales muted inside her. There were many, many trapped stories and these stories had agents in them that, when put in a vat, would boil and boil. And could that cauldron bubble!

He would take care of her when the trouble activated that cauldron inside her—or rather when her release valve was inconsistent. He didn't do his work from home for all these months for nothing. He had put aside enough money where either hospitalization or taking a pay cut amounted to the same financially. He chose staying home and *being* the help. Sometimes he wondered if he made a difference at all.

He snuggled close to her making sure his face wasn't directly inhaling her sangria breath. She tried not to laugh too much as she told him what had happened. The level of amusement was sized more by the wine than by the primer of humor.

Lately, she didn't coat his house with gaiety very often.

Chapter 28

Ceci had enjoyed talking to Tim tonight. She was right about sangria. *Sangue*, blood. That's what happened. It gave her blood and strength to talk.

"Isn't it easier to just take the attendance?"

"If you have a penchant for banality," she said. That daily chore was very boring to Ceci, so she pretended to take attendance. She would skim the room and two feats would be accomplished. She appeared like a responsible teacher who remembered to take attendance promptly. And she could impress the kids that she knew everybody's name. She could never let the kids realize that well into the school year she still didn't know their names. They had taken a major exam and Ginger Dennehy came up to the desk.

"I was absent yesterday when you gave out the grades. What did I get on the test? I studied so hard." Ceci spun the gradebook over to Ginger and opened to the page.

"I'm busy now, but... er...find your name and look for it, okay?" Ginger traveled her finger down the column to her name and quickly saw her grade. Must be getting old, Ceci thought, because she couldn't see upside down as well as she used to and couldn't tell on which row Ginger stopped to see the grade.

The all-knowing Mrs. McKinney wasn't going to be beaten, not by an innocent child who would never think that a teacher still didn't know her students yet. Would she think her teacher had no idea which grade belonged to whom?

"So what did you think you got?" Ceci asked. Her next question would be determined by Ginger's answer.

"At least ten points higher." The game was getting rough and Ceci had to limber up.

"Why don't you put a little pencil mark near it to remind me to check it out later on."

"Okay," said Ginger. It always worked. What a champ Ceci was. She could dupe anybody she wanted to any time she wanted.

Ceci realized that she didn't have to make the decision. Now, her life was in Plan B. It had gotten to a point where she rarely tried Plan A. It took too much effort to live her life with total honesty. Sometimes when she was honest, she found that it was like spitting up in the air. Her sputum somehow did not begin with the powerful trajectory it used to. When the spittle descended, she no longer had time to run away from it. Now she looked at it and almost waited for it to be the human doo dropping on her windshield. Unfortunately, the cracks in the windshield protecting her psyche were getting wider and becoming irreparable and she didn't have time to go to a glazier. And she didn't have that many days in her sick bank to waste waiting for someone to repair it.

"Do you think these kids will ever figure out that you do not know who they are yet?" Tim asked.

"Well, I certainly know the bad ones. Those I know twenty minutes into class the first day," she said.

He looked at Ceci. "Tell me...how you are feeling."

"You mean twenty minutes took too long?"

"How are you feeling?" he repeated.

For some reason she didn't mind his probing.

"Well, I am feeling just fine and dandy. No, correction, I am feeling particularly dandy and randy. Hey, I made a poem." She laughed and he let himself join her as she spit out the wine staining the front of her blouse.

"Dandy and randy. Yes, that rhymes," he said enjoying some uncomplicated humor with her. It felt good. "Maybe you could be an English teacher when you get big."

They both laughed the silly laugh of two people on a couch, one buzzed and one longing for something to laugh about. They held each other after he managed to take the glass from her, reach across and place the glass on the end table. He fell onto her after she tickled him under his outstretched arm. He hated that he was so ticklish and she enjoyed that about him. People who were ticklish connoted a kind of innocence that she liked and didn't have. When someone tickled her, she felt violated and demanded that the person stop. She could not equate tickling with fun. She always felt that laughter from fun came as a result of hearing or seeing something humorous. You did not laugh if someone touched a certain part of your body. You could do the same thing to a dog and if it knew how to laugh, would it? But she was not a dog.

No matter what her mother believed.

He finger combed her hair and it still had the softness he so loved. He waited until the spell subsided and said,

"Some nasty cough you got there, huh?"

"What cough?" she said.

Chapter 29

Tim had a hard time keeping up with Ceci and her polar moods. When she walked into the house, he never knew which wife would be entering.

"She's burning out," Margot said and he would agree with his wife's best friend because he liked thinking Ceci's behavior was that simple to diagnose. He didn't mind discussing Ceci with Margot because he knew she generally loved his wife. He called the moods tantrums because it made it easier for him not to worry about her so much. His professional analysis told him otherwise. It would just be a matter of time until he had to take a stronger approach.

For now, she was still functioning. A lot of her erratic behavior—the occasional stuttering, the limping, mannerisms of other people—could be attributed to the stress her job normally involved, but perhaps now magnified.

In spite of what was happening to Ceci, Tim could still search through the files of his memory and pull out a folder—a Ceci-made-him-pee-his-pants folder—that could encourage him not to quit on her.

The edges of those folders were so worn soft from handling that he had to be very careful when he grabbed for them. He only needed to skim through the contents because he knew them all by heart.

His favorite was the time they took a day trip to New York City and visited the NBC Studios store.

"Timothy, we still have six minutes until the tour. Got to make tinkees."

"Okay. Hurry up. I'll wait outside."

"You mean you won't wait in the stall with me? All the other husbands do," she pouted.

"Would you get the flow going. The minutes are dripping by."

"Like my tinkees, Daddy? Well, okay for you," she said. "When you have trouble getting your pantyhose off, don't you come crying to me."

She was out in two minutes and neither one of them knew where the meeting place for the tour was. She approached a help-person in a blue uniform standing at attention, legs apart slightly and hands on hips. His smile welcomed her question.

"Excuse me, sir. Where is the meeting place for the tour?" He just stared at her, still smiling and still loving his job.

"We're in quite a hurry," she said. "Tour starts in a couple of minutes. Where do they meet?"

Now this man was annoying Ceci. His painted smile was passive aggression, she was sure of it. His smile was the Bartleby, the Scrivener smile saying "I'd prefer not to" as Herman Melville's Bartleby always said. Bartleby had an excuse. He worked in the dead letter office of a New York post office in the 1800s so his answering, "I'd prefer not to" to anyone who directed him to do a chore made sense to Ceci. She always wondered if Bartleby became that way *after* he got the job or did he get the job because he was so suited?

She approved of Bartleby, but she disapproved of this smiling idiot pretending that he was there to help the customers of NBC Studios. The rest of the customers walked by him and politely smiled at Ceci while snickering at him.

Ceci was not to be discouraged. The girls behind the counter selling mementos to other visitors of the studio stared at her. To hell with them, Ceci thought. She was not going to let this guy get away with not doing his job. Maybe they didn't care, but she did.

"Smile away, jerko." She stomped directly up to him and put her face up to his smooth and shiny visage. This time she was going to look into his eyes, not just at his contrived, phony pleasant—but not fooling Ceci for one minute—whole body stance.

When she poked him, he sprang back and forth with a boing the way those cardboard life-sized cut-outs sway in the wind at the gas station pumps. He must have been related to the guy who says you can win a million bucks if you buy a lottery ticket after buying gas. The cardboard guy you have to be careful not to hit with your car when you park ever so close to the pump so you don't have to stretch the hose too much and risk scraping the car.

She could feel her face become hot and most likely very red. She hated when that happened because she felt like her face had been disloyal to her, had made it impossible to keep walking as if nothing had happened. It precluded any possibility that she could get away without being embarrassed about doing something this stupid. Bad enough she was seen talking to a cardboard man, but she was seen getting *angry* at a cardboard man. The ultimate indignity was that a cardboard man was laughing at her while she was scolding him.

Tim couldn't remember when they both hooted so much. Even that cardboard guy looked like his brushed on smile was broader than it was when she asked him for directions to go on a tour which was to begin in a couple of minutes.

"Got any markers with you?" Tim managed.

"Got my school ones. What color do you need?"

"Black'll do." After Tim drew the smile wider and darkened a few front teeth on the man, their laughing was so uncontrollable that they decided to find another bathroom.

At another television studio.

Preferably in another city.

Chapter 30

The name Cecilia Scarpelli-McKinney always sounded ridiculous to her. There was an argument every time Gilda visited Ceci. Gilda would notice the mail and how it was addressed to Ceci.

"Why are you ashamed of your last name? A lot of professionals use a hyphenated name. It will make you sound important. And what is so wrong with Cecilia? It was my mother's name," Gilda Scarpelli said.

"How come you don't use Gilda Minzo-Scarpelli?"

Gilda didn't even have to think of a retort. "I would if I needed to feel important."

At 75 years old, Gilda still maintained a svelte figure, black hair, which she swore she never dyed, and the same vibrancy as when she was a straightforward, no-nonsense teen. Her very presence could inject cyclonic activity in a room leaving quite a whirlwind.

"Are you sure you put enough pork in that gravy? Nothing worse than bland sauce over linguine. But then again, you are all used to it, I guess."

"We're doing just fine, Mom," Tim would say.

Using banter, Tim could always diffuse Gilda when she was winding up.

"You know Mom, when you last visited the White House with all the rules and regulations, all the high official protocol, all the secretive, protective atmosphere of the most important building in the world, did you leave it a hut bordering on a hubble?"

"Go ahead. You can both do what you want. I can eat anything. It's the children I am thinking about."

"You could always bring the food," Ceci suggested.

"I would, but you might not like it. I cook healthy."

Jaime and Jimmy loved their grandmother.

"Grandma, you got a new iPod. What was wrong with your old one?"

"Not enough memory," Gilda said as she showed Jaime the new mp3 player which matched her new cell phone.

"You got a different cell phone, too?" Jimmy said.

"Can't have people gossiping that my stuff doesn't match," Gilda said as Jimmy gave her a bear hug.

Jaime's friends loved Gilda, also, and they preferred staying at Jaime's grandmother's than at Jaime's house because they said her grandma was cool. Jaime preferred going to Gilda because she completely spoiled her granddaughter. In Gilda's eyes, Jaime was perfect. Jaime could be rude to her mother and Gilda would rationalize the behavior.

"Well, what did you do to her that made her talk that way to you?" she'd ask Ceci more as a rhetorical question than a serious inquiry, but she would tell Jaime—without Ceci's hearing—that she should speak more kindly to her mom, but she didn't say it with as much enthusiasm as she knew she should.

Gilda likewise adored her granddaughter. When Jaime was a little girl, Gilda would remind her that they each owned the other's heart. One Christmas when Jaime was seven, she was very excited at buying her own gifts from the school's annual Holiday shopping event.

"Wait 'til you see what I got you, Grandma. You're gonna love it."

"I have to love it; you're my Jaime."

When Christmas Eve arrived and everybody finally could allow themselves to get excited as the clock bonged midnight, Jaime—not the least bit affected by the late hour—ran up to her grandmother and demanded she open her gift first.

"Only if you open mine next," said Gilda.

"Okay, okay. Here," she said and pushed the present into Gilda's hands. She did just as Jaime asked and anxiously tore open the gift and fumbled in clumsy anticipation until she opened the box. Jaime's eyes widened more than it seemed possible and focused on Gilda's reaction. Gilda's smile supplied as much light as the Star of Bethlehem guiding the Three Kings. She took out the metal heart dangling from an inexpensive and much too short chain and placed it around her neck. Eyes welling, she told Jaime to open hers.

"Hurry, hurry, you slow poke."

With much squealing from Jaime and more tears from Gilda, Jaime took out a gold heart pendant hanging from a 14 karat gold chain and placed it near her chest.

"Sweetheart, let Grandma put it on for you." Gilda whispered in Jaime's ear, "now we *really* have each other's heart."

"But the one you gave me shines more than the one I gave you, Grandma."

"Oh, no it doesn't, my beautiful granddaughter. They shine exactly same. They are our hearts."

Ceci had many reasons for not using a hyphenated name. She could both rankle her mother and she could hide completely behind Tim. Ceci McKinney sounded safer than Cecilia Scarpelli-McKinney. Tim liked shielding his wife either physically or with his surname.

"Marriage certificates give power to men," she would tease Tim.

"Okay, Ms. Scarpelli…"

"Hey, watch that."

Tim felt his marriage certificate was assurance that someone loved him.

When Gilda came over, Ceci needed to think of Tim so she could be mentally swept away from her mother. She reflected back to when she first met Tim. It was at a party in Holbrook, Long Island. Theirs was a unique meeting, although to Ceci house parties weren't necessarily unique. Cocktail parties always bored Ceci, but all her friends were going to this one.

"Come on, Cee. Going to be a lot of cute guys," they said. It was a kind of unlabeled singles party and no one really admitted it. They went under the guise that the church was sponsoring it and Rosemarie, 26 and single, had her own house and sure, she said, it would be no trouble to have the party here. Very plain looking and not able to attract men, housing a singles party was the only guaranteed way she would see men, or better yet, have men see her. Everybody talked to the hostess. It worked beautifully for Rosemarie. She donated the wine and cheese and the dessert. It was her court and whatever she served was hailed.

Ceci wondered why the guests were all congregating in the kitchen. Standing around the large refrigerator with the freezer on the bottom, the guests complimented Rosemarie on her Chihuahua.

The freaking dog is named Albert, Ceci thought, but said aloud with the other admirers, "Oh he is soo adorable. Look at his cute brown eyes. I could just cuddle him to pieces."

Albert yapped incessantly at the guests who had formed a kind of a circle. Ceci went along with the crowd and agreed with all their compliments for the tiny brown feisty canine with the bulging eyes.

"What a gorgeous doggie you are, yes."

"Look at how you are protecting your mommy."

"Be careful, now, and let Mommy get more ice."

"Oh, look, you are showing us your beautiful teeth."

"I'd like to kick it into the freezer," Tim whispered to

Ceci. She snapped out of party pretense, turned around and saw good looking Tim, the ventriloquist, through smiling face, repeat,

"I'd like to kick that little rat into the freezer."

That was it. Ceci knew this was the man she was going to marry. They left the party early, dated for a year and were wed on June 22.

Just like that.

Chapter 31

Ceci didn't know who could be funnier, she or Tim. He could make her laugh when the entire world was weeping. He could poke fun and say things about people and not really mean them. He could say nice things about her and she hoped he meant them.

Except for this year. Everything was different this year. She chose to blame Tim for everything. He'd let her, so why not. It was his fault that literary characters were beginning to take over her psyche; it was his fault that she'd forget what she was saying mid-sentence; it was his fault she wore a strait jacket, just in case.

"Somebody has to pay and I choose you, Timothy McKinney," she said. Was he not listening, she wondered, or does he just not hear me? I know I am talking. I must be; I can hear me clearly.

Tim was always respectful to and tolerant of Gilda. He knew the tension that was created any time Gilda and Ceci were in the same room. This Christmas Eve was going to be monumental in level of stress. That was the night that no one really said what he or she felt. All the appropriate festive sentiments were shared. All the standard Christmas songs were sung and Tim performed the traditional reading of Clement C. Moore's "A Visit from St. Nicholas." The kids were grown, but it would not have felt like Christmas if Tim didn't read that story to them. He'd shut the lights and read by candlelight. That was the only guaranteed time that Gilda and Ceci would behave themselves. Jaime and Jimmy especially waited for that time because they were assured there would be ambient silence with only Daddy reading about Jolly Old St. Nick with his little round belly that shook when he laughed like a bowlful of jelly.

Tim didn't really care if his teenage kids were absorbing that children's story or not, but he understood and appreciated their need to hear it. He took his time during the narrative and exaggerated certain sections, finger dancing the sugar plums and winking his eye ensuring that the kids had nothing to dread. He knew how much they craved some quiet, loving time. Time when Gilda was not hacking into Ceci was good for them.

Jaime and Jimmy excused Gilda's behavior because they genuinely found her entertaining. She said the things they wouldn't normally verbalize, but wanted to. At 17, Jaime was not as loath to utter the same to her own mother, while Jimmy controlled any urges to be sarcastic to Ceci. It was more than feeling it would not be polite; he really didn't want to hurt his mother.

Gilda didn't insult Tim too much, but she still managed to offer her unsolicited opinion. "So, what's been happening around the home front, Timothy, my favorite son-in-law?"

"Everything's good, Mom. And I am your *only* son-in-law."

"Then why don't you answer my calls? You know I am wor…interested in knowing what goes on in the McKinney house. My grandkids live there, you know. Not that my daughter is breaking down my door to visit me."

Tim decided that he would make sure Christmas Eve was a good one. You never knew what was going to happen when Gilda visited. When his father-in-law Gino Scarpelli was alive, he could control his wife.

Sometimes Tim wondered what he, himself, was doing wrong that he couldn't control Ceci as effectively. Maybe it was because Gino felt that Gilda was as soft as absorbent cotton. She was a round fluffy, cotton ball. Ceci was a round cotton ball, also. Only with Ceci there was a needle inside it and even though the ball was pretty and soft to look at, if squeezed too hard, there would be much pain as in the Taoist allegory of the hidden needle in the cotton ball.

Ceci was Tim's cotton ball. He could lift it and gently take it with him. He could roll it as long as he didn't push into it too hard. He could toss it and it would bounce off walls. What could get tricky was if it bounced too hard onto someone, that someone could get an unwelcomed pinch. If he got careless and really threw the cotton ball hard against something, the force of its hitting that something and ricocheting back to him could prick him. What, then, could he use to apply any kind of salve? He wouldn't trust just any cotton balls in the medicine cabinet.

To avoid any problems, it was better to just leave the cotton ball alone and let it sit there looking pretty.

Chapter 32

Unlike today, when Ceci was a small child, she did not feel so abused or disappointed. Double yolk eggs became an important part of her childhood. One would crack open an egg and there would either be a single yolk—most of the time—or there would be a bonus, a double yolk. Her mother was sure that city supermarkets never sold double yolks. You could only find them on chicken farms.

Finding a double yolk was the beginning of a beautiful experience that lingered until bedtime when it was mentioned again. Ceci didn't know if it were she or her mother who loved them more. It didn't matter; it was love experienced by mother and daughter—a rare emotion for Ceci in her adult life.

Ceci only saw double yolks when she and Gilda spent the summers in their bungalow in Selden, Long Island. Because of their jobs, Gino and Alan would stay at home in Brooklyn and visit on weekends. These were the times before they had a telephone in the bungalow and from Monday through Friday morning, Gilda belonged to Ceci. From Friday evening until Sunday, Gilda was Gino's.

"Oh, oh. Looks like we have a double yolker, baby," Gilda would say examining the large egg, turning it this way and that. It didn't really matter if the egg was a real double yolk or not. Just Gilda's thinking it might be meant it *was* to Ceci. It was the ritual that Ceci longed for and Gilda never disappointed her.

Disappointment and disapproval from Gilda didn't begin until Ceci became an adult. It seemed like Gilda enjoyed doling out her criticism to Ceci. She took her time with it. Was it unpleasant? Was it distasteful? Was it both? Bingo. Gilda would give the next dose and she would administer it without a spoonful of sugar. Oh, the medicine would go down all right. It would go down.

"Mother-in-law of mine," Tim would begin. Gilda didn't know why, but she could be tempered by Tim. He was not the paragon of sons-in-law, by any means. He was not as strong or as gentle as her husband Gino; he was not as aware of Gilda's quirks; he was *not* Gino Scarpelli. That was good.

In actuality, Gino was the unique one, not Gilda. To the world, Gilda was the one who was never to be duplicated; she was the one who was the strong one of the pair; she was the one who made all the decisions. That was true overtly.

Gino was unassumed, quiet dignity. He was strength that didn't need to prove it existed. He had kindness and honesty which vicariously lent to the uniqueness that Gilda was known for. Gino was a tall burly man who was as gentle in personality as he was rough looking. With soft dark straight hair, bright brown eyes and deep chin cleft, a handsomeness could still be seen even in his later years.

"Look at that face," Gilda would say stroking it and outlining his graying mustache. "Did Clark Gable have anything over my Gino? I do not think so."

Gilda was not as educated as Ceci and was not exposed to the same circles as her daughter for which Ceci was grateful. Gilda in her loudness embarrassed Ceci. Gilda in her aggressiveness and oblivion of how she appeared to people made Ceci constantly ashamed of her mother. It never affected Gilda, though. Indifferent to Ceci's feelings, Gilda behaved any way she felt like.

Gilda was the person Ceci hated. Loved. Ran from. Appreciated. Believed. Ridiculed. Cried for—in secret. Gilda's was the strength Ceci would never have although nobody knew that.

Tim was the only person, beside his father-in-law, who was least intimidated by Gilda and her actions. What placed Tim high on the ladder in Gilda's view was that he was honest in his approach to her. And he wasn't cruel. It was the top rung he was not allowed to reach. They both knew only Gino and Alan used it.

Ceci never even tried.

Chapter 33

While Gino was alive, Gilda was different personalities. Most people were amused by her. Relatives wondered and worried how Gilda would fare without her husband and his patience, understanding and strength.

They sat in the hospital waiting room.

"Mom is normally a loose cannon," Ceci said to Alan. That image, though overused, Ceci thought, was more precise than any other applied to her mother. Gilda was like a 32-pounder cannon on the lower deck of an armed man o' war. If separated from the other cannons, there was no telling what damage it could do. Ceci imagined that the cannon would roll this way and that, missing this, hitting that. Sometimes, a cannonball might drop out of it and the sound of the thud would be deafening to the people on board this ship. It would be a loud noise, but not too destructive. Just like Gilda.

Gino was the captain of the ship who made sure the cannons were always secured. Ceci was certain that if cannons had thoughts and emotions, they would listen to Gino.

Ceci could feel the menacing pressure in her chest. It was as if that pressure wanted to exit her back to start applying the pressure again. She was Sisyphus rolling that rock up the hill only to have it roll back down when he reached the top. She was Prometheus having his liver eaten by day, regenerating at night to be gnawed at again by day. She was being punished by her Zeus, Gilda.

Gino had suffered a massive heart attack and the doctors made it clear he would not live the night. Gilda had brought him in at 3 pm and eight hours remained in the waiting room, motionless. She imagined that people came to her and offered her food, offered her a blanket. They had to have; she couldn't have just sat there. The doctors came out at 11:30 and sat on either side of her.

"Don't say anything to me. What do you know? You don't know my Gino," she wanted to say. Gilda knew what had happened. She understood. By refusing to accept the truth, her husband lingered a little longer in her world. She still had that little bit of strength left to keep Gino alive a few more minutes.

"Don't anybody touch me," she said as if they would pull her away from Gino's spirit. She would never release him without a battle.

Gino would understand, but he would also gently nudge her. "Go ahead, mi amore. You go with the children."

Ceci, Tim and Alan approached her. Ceci and Tim escorted her to the car a half hour later. Alan would take care of the hospital paper work.

During Gino's wake, Tim tried to be attentive to his mother-in-law while Ceci sat on the same settee, watching her mother stare ahead. She visited all the places Gilda must have visited and said all the same things as her mother did to anybody who tried to comfort her.

At no time, did Gilda behave harshly or thoughtlessly to Jaime and Jimmy. At no time did she ever forget to apply the love she had on those two kids. She was the thick salve her grandchildren needed. She knew the places of injury and she knew how much and how often the application. She knew just how much they needed at the loss of their grandpa and they knew their grandma would help them. It was this atmosphere of shared love that excused any inappropriate comments, any out-moded phrases, any grandma-isms. That mutually valuable relationship extended to Tim, as well, though much more measured.

Ceci shared nothing of Gilda's offerings to the rest of the family. Ceci didn't seem to want it and her mother didn't want to share it. Ceci didn't seem to need it and Gilda was glad because she really had no idea how to help Ceci if she ever did ask for help. It would have been kind of nice to have a daughter to laugh with, to be silly with, to cry with.

If Gilda saw a tear on Ceci or what might have appeared like a tear, Gilda would not know what to do because she didn't think Ceci was emotionally capable of weeping. If she detected that strange-appearing lachrymose drop, she would be unnerved. Gilda might think it came from somewhere else. And then what would she do?

But that was not an issue to be contended with. Ceci never disappointed Gilda in that way. Maybe there were no tear ducts. No, no, that wasn't it. People were born with tear ducts.

Gilda always thought anybody could cry.

Chapter 34

Ceci loved Christmas Eve, but she also loved when it was over. The end of the holiday meant Gilda was going home. She wanted her to be there; she wanted her to leave.

This conundrum was with Ceci her whole life. It was most likely from the second she was slapped by the doctor and ordered to inhale for the first time. Ceci wondered if the doctors really did hold the babies by one hand, dangle them and slap with their other hand. Couldn't the baby just begin inhaling on its own? She hoped that is what happened to her. This way she could believe that she was in control of her life from second one. If that were the case, then, did Gilda demand that first breath to be taken all over again?

She wanted to blame Gilda's mercurial personality on Alan. She wanted her brother to take the blame the way he always did when Gilda was after her. Alan would stand in front of Ceci blocking her from Gilda's railings. Alan would dodge some blows or accept them buffering the strikes meant for Ceci. Alan absorbed everything unpleasant that was meant for Ceci. She was the brat; she was the one answering her mother back; she was the heartless one who would stop at nothing—short of hurting her dad—to wound and defame her mother.

Ceci did not show her feelings about her mother to the outside world. To herself, she would chastise, malign and spit at her mother when the only audience was Ceci. That audience judged, passed sentence, watched the punishment inflicted on Ceci by judge Ceci. The TV cameraman Ceci would show scorn for the prisoner and join in on the sneering of the rest of the world inhabited by Ceci.

Ceci didn't know who loved Alan more, Gilda or she. Gilda would think it was she because he was her son. That was enough of a reason for any mother, Ceci guessed. Ceci knew it was she because Alan was her salvation, her link to goodness, her pipeline to sanity in the world of Ceci.

Alan was comfortable in any environment Ceci created. He could visit it or live in it for as long as Ceci wanted or needed. When he decided to succumb to lung cancer, he damaged her heart leaving a void she was trying unsuccessfully to fill with the lifestyle she led now. She used to take dry runs of what it would be like if her brother ever died. Even while he was dying, she was positive he would never die. He couldn't. What would she do without him? How could she fend off Gilda?

Gilda had mellowed much since Alan's death. She never spoke of him to her daughter. She would not share the severe pain and raw sadness she felt at the loss of her child. She didn't have Gino to help bear it the way she had Alan to help bear the loss of her husband. She only had Ceci and she accepted that Ceci had no use for her. She and Ceci didn't talk about each other's feelings. Why waste each other's time talking about important things. Surface conversation was so much easier.

"Bye, Mom. Did you have a nice time?" asked Ceci.

"Of course. I always do. Where are those fantastic kids?"

"Bye, Grandma. Love you tons," said Jaime holding her tight and laughing at how muffled her grandmother's voice was as she kept telling Jaime how gorgeous she was and how she would miss her so much.

"Where's my big grandson, that handsome devil?"

"Bye, Grams," Jimmy said and bear hugged her again. She was unsuccessful at breaking free because she was not really trying that hard.

"Tim, great meal, great story-telling."

"Stay well, Mom."

As the car pulled away, Ceci could feel relief pushing down, dissipating her headache and settling in her legs making it so easy to sink into her recliner. Her shoulders got lighter and she felt like she would float away.

"Too bad I can't wish my mother gone so I could have this feeling forever," she said.

"Want another demi-tasse of coffee and a cannoli?" Tim knew exactly which comfort food to offer his wife when his wife was suspended over some very deadly chasm.

"Don't really care."

He brought her a cup of espresso with a chocolate-dipped cannoli. She bit into the pastry savoring the cool mixture of crunchy chocolate sweetness and creamy casata filling. She avoided the much-needed espresso because Gilda had made it. She chose iced water, instead, and was angry that she had to settle for something she really didn't want. The espresso with black sambuca would have gone perfectly with the cannoli.

"That woman always ruins everything," Ceci said.

Chapter 35

The Alcmene High School general office had only been open for twenty minutes and the air was still cold. When Ceci signed in, she could feel an uncertainty. What's wrong now, she thought. She went to her mailbox and saw the familiar pink telephone message with a "please see me" checked off. It was a joke among the other teachers to get one of these in the mailbox. The proverbial cliché pink slip. Louise, the principal's secretary, was free with giving out the blank pads to mischievous teachers like Ceci.

Everyone knew what Ceci was up to whenever she asked for a new pad. She was very liberal in distributing the See Me's to other colleagues. They waited for them. She was expert at forging other administrators' signatures. She sent one to Frieda, the Spanish teacher, who provoked the Right Guard to fight, but always overcame the deodorant in battle. Frieda received a See Me suggesting she try another brand which contained pelletized lime. There were See Me's in mailboxes sent from the superintendent, from Mother Theresa, from the mayor of Camden, NJ, and from Oprah. One time after sending out several See Me's in one week, she received one that had a second pink sheet stapled to the first. Page one said

See Me and page two was a picture of someone mooning. Ceci didn't know of anyone else who could forge the principal's name. Oh sure, there were forgers of the forger, but Ceci could always tell whose handwriting it was.

But not this day. This one really stumped her. Holding the telephone message, Ceci pretended that she was trembling as she approached Louise's desk. Louise and Ceci had been friends since Prospect Heights High School in Brooklyn. They each knew when the other was playing a practical joke. This time Louise was really good. Ceci could detect nothing.

"Hey Lulu, whut up?" For a second Ceci thought Louise might be upset.

"Lou?"

"He wants you to go straight in," her friend said trying to look as though she had to file something very important.

"You are not suggesting that I should cut the line on all these people who have been waiting for an audience with the Holy Father," Ceci said and looked at Louise's head until she turned it and was forced to look straight into Ceci's face.

"Why don't you go right in, Cee."

Ceci was about to knock on the open door when Cornelius Jackson said, "just come in Mrs. McKinney, please."

"Mrs. McKinney, hmm, well, okay *Mr. Cornelius Jackson*," she said. She went in and obediently sat opposite him. Neil Jackson took out his pen and rolled it back and forth between his thumb and index finger, from his index finger, through his ring finger and back again to begin re-lacing it through his fingers. This he did adroitly over and over again. Instead of annoying Ceci, it mesmerized her. She could swear she was going to fall asleep, but knew how ridiculous that would be. As soon as she became aware of her thinking that she was dozing off and wanting to laugh at herself for even thinking that, Neil's voice got louder.

"Ceci? Ceci!"

"I'm still here, Your Holiness."

"How are you doing today?"

"As opposed to which day?" she asked.

He said nothing and waited a few seconds. "Do you know long we've been friends?"

"Oh now, don't tell me you want a divorce?" She smiled and waited for his smile which didn't appear.

"30 years," he said.

"The kids. The kids. How will we tell the kids?"

"You okay?" Neil said.

"I'm okay. You're okay. Good, glad we got that out of the way. No sexually transmitted diseases between us. Whew, I feel better already. Can I go now?"

"We are all worried about you."

"But I've been using the ointment and the outbursts are going away. It's your fault for not wearing a condom."

Ceci was surprised that Neil did not react the way he usually did, with a burst that made Ceci laugh more. She was the only one who could make him laugh when things were not that funny.

She recalled once needing to get a picture of him and none of the shots she had taken seemed good enough for the yearbook principal's page. She just couldn't get him to sport that Dennis Quaid smile she loved so much. She aimed the camera at him and he simply stared at the lens.

"Imagine Frieda spread eagle just waiting for you to ravish her." Nobody could picture 81-year-old Frieda Seadau who absolutely refused to retire, let alone use deordorant, and would teach school until the educational process of teachers in a building with kids was passé. Frieda had a voice that could outscream Coach Kenny Richards. She would wear the same clothes three days in a row and become indignant when the kids would hold their noses as they passed. She could gum through her sandwich while her teeth were soaking in Polident at her desk. It was a mental image that he could not see without spitting out his Juicy Fruit gum. The trajectory hit Ceci and they both laughed. At least she got that great picture she wanted. Only they would know what she had to say to get that perfect smile under the 14 pt. headlined Principal's Message box.

A half hour later Ceci left Neil's office. She passed Louise and didn't even need to shun her as Louise was making herself very busy.

So, she knows what the damned meet-up was about, thought Ceci. Of course she would. People casually said good morning to Ceci and she nodded to each. The young department members would give a swashbuckling bow and swirl their plumed musketeer hats if they had them. They performed that regally and she accepted it majestically as any queen would.

There were no yardsticks from which to measure people's honest reactions to Ceci and whatever behavior Tim and now Neil were hinting was developing. She was getting tired of their evasiveness.

Speak up, fools, she thought.

Then again, she always thought this.

Chapter 36

It was the first day back from the winter break and although Ceci was tired, she was anxious to get to work. She was in her own court and she alone reigned. Gilda was probably home calling her friends to organize lunches over which she would relay just how horrible her daughter was. She would most likely compare her offspring—the one who was alive and the one who died. Why not? She did lose a prize of a pup and was left with the runt of the litter.

"Screw her," she said aloud. Ceci was very brave when Gilda was not around.

"Good morning, my little chickadees," Ceci said. First period class grunted their good mornings, checked the board for the homework assignment and took their seats.

"What are we doing today?" Mari in the second row asked.

"Nothing."

"Oh good. When do we start?"

"Any time."

"Wait, wait," the girl in front of Mari said. "I gotta catch up."

Ceci nodded, validating their attempts at joking. Actually, she *did* find this class funny and they felt the same about her.

"I have an idea. Want to watch a movie?"

"Yeah," they said together, now truly alert.

She took one of the DVDs she had forgotten to file from two weeks ago and held it up.

"You see it?" and she put it in the drawer. "How'd you like it?"

"Duh," they said.

"Want to see the movie again," she asked ready to take the DVD out of the drawer.

"Okay then, take out your homework." This class was the easiest of her schedule. They did their assignments on time. They understood and appreciated her jokes; they weren't afraid to tease her; they were all bright. She never needed to consult her planbook other than the one glance at the beginning of the period reminding her of what she was up to. The first forty-two minutes of her day always passed without incident. Periods two and three completed the assigned work complaining that she always gave so much homework and didn't she realize they just came back from Christmas and they were sooo tired. Boy, school's lousy.

Marshall's class was the litmus test and although it was rewarding, it was stressful and she always welcomed her lunch break which she relished alone using the excuse that she had yearbook work to do.

Ever using the yearbook as her way to get the amenities privy to teachers who were advisors of the more difficult clubs, her room was her private second home complete with refrigerator, microwave, coffeemaker, all sectioned off by extra file cabinets which functioned as a room divider. She even taped bulletin board paper onto the back of the cabinets to create a decorative wall of her "office."

In order to allay any jealousy of the other teachers, each amenity had an explainable reason for being in the room. The refrigerator kept film fresh even though she had been taking digital candid shots of the students for more than a decade. In case the students wanted to work during their lunch periods (which they never did), they needed to keep their lunches fresh. When the kids stayed until at least five o'clock, they had to have something to eat and something warmed in a microwave was better than sandwiches (which they never ate). In order to be kept alert for the students, freshly-brewed coffee was a necessity. As chairperson, as well as advisor to the biggest fundraiser of the school, she needed extra file cabinets

Inside her office were another desk, a cushioned chair, the teacher wardrobe closet, and a door leading to the back courtyard. Even when the yearbook was done, she enjoyed her office/apartment.

She decided to eat her lunch casually and not do anything yearbook-related. After all, it *was* the first day back from vacation. When the kids were right, they were right. She took off her shoes, put her feet on top of the desk and leaned the chair back a bit and managed her pen—through the thumb, to the index finger, through the middle finger, ring finger and back again.

Chapter 37

Thank goodness for crazy kids, Ceci thought. Crazy students and their antics were what kept her buoyant on the *snot-green sea* which was her life. It always irritated her that James Joyce in *Ulysses* played on Homer's *wine-dark sea* in *The Odyssey*. Joyce was a great enough author. Ceci was not as great a writer as Joyce, so she could use the pun.

Eighth period was not a bad group. Sometimes they would be tired from the day and a bit listless. Good for her because she was wound up and sugar infused so close after lunch. It was bad for her because today, they were in great lively form.

She chose to take advantage of the alertness of the class. She knew the mythology unit scheduled soon was going to be a challenge for her as well as for the kids. She decided to whet their appetites for some Greek literary food and let them savor one of the more popular stories in preparation for the complete unit. All kids enjoyed the tale of the Cyclopes.

About three quarters through an especially productive lesson for Ceci, they were finally sailing along with Odysseus in spite of the *in medias res* timeline that so confused the students and the newer teachers.

"How come the story starts in the middle?" a student would ask.

"You mean *in medias res*? It's all Greek to me, too," Ceci would say, enjoying the joke even though they did not get it.

Ceci conducted her life in medias res, in the middle of things, and until recently, she had been doing fine.

She had been pleased with the progress of the class discussion/lecture when a student raised her hand. She used to welcome questions which could be teaching aids to avert a guaranteed lesson in ennui. She did not need this kid interrupting some real live learning. Nevertheless, her hand was up and Ceci stopped the lecture.

"Yes, Allison?"

"What's today's date?"

"Doesn't matter," Ceci answered hoping to go back to the lesson not breaking its continuity. The hand went up again. Trying not to look too annoyed, Ceci stopped and asked in a lower voice, "Yes, Allison?"

"What's today's date?"

She was surprised that Allison, a diminutive quiet soul who would only interrupt if she really *needed* an answer, was persistent. Ceci tried to moderate her response.

"Allison, it doesn't matter what the date is. You are just listening to this lesson—which is going on famously, might I add—and there is no writing involved. And anyway, the day is almost over. Okay? So let's continue."

Allison's hand went up still again and Ceci was going to put a stop to the question.

"What is it?"

"What's today's date?" said Allison. Ceci was surprised at how agitated she was getting while Allison's questions remained monotoned.

"March Fourth," she yelled. At that moment everything was in slow motion for Ceci as the students, one by one, came up to the front of the room. First row, second row, and on. After about two minutes of organized walking in step, the entire class was now standing at the front of the room. She knew something was up. Duh, as the kids would have said. She knew they were playing a joke on her and she knew she *had* to figure it out—fast. It took her ten seconds which transformed into ten hours.

She searched her inventory of Ceci Silly Stunts which her students loved. This was one she didn't recognize, let alone use. She looked at the clock. Ten minutes left until the end of the period. She looked at her clothes. No chalk on her blazer. A quick look at the door window's reflection. Her hair was in place and there was no evidence from her last sneezing attack. No mosquitoes out so no mosquito bite scabs scratched leaving blood to peek through her blouse. Her shoes matched. A two second scan. Kids lined up. It was the wrong period for a repeat of Marshall's birthday party.

These were good kids who were playing a joke on her and she didn't get it. She would *never* live this down. Falling off a chair was one thing, but not understanding a joke and being the butt of it was not an option. It was not like Ceci not to catch on, not to be able to respond the very next second. I must be losing it, she thought. She only gave herself five seconds more until concession. It would only be fair to herself and to them.

Time for an emergency rapid evaluation. Kids walked in cadence, pounding the floor at the same time, intentionally. Organized. Soldier-like. Marching. To the teacher's desk. Coming forth. Marching forth. Damn!! Those stinkers. Ceci looked at the date—March 4th.

She stopped and all the kids understood her look of recognition of the joke, of her concession, of her appreciation of their antics. They probably also understood that she liked them. She looked at Allison, the kid who was usually nondescript and unpopular. Allison wasn't hated, ostracized or even disliked; it was worse. She was unnoticed and that's precisely why the class selected her. Did they realize that Allison, boring, blah-looking Allison, would shine today?

For a long time Allison would be the referent of these kids if ever they related to their own children how they, themselves, behaved when they were kids. Teachers in the faculty room that day would laugh about it. Subsequent teachers in subsequent faculty rooms would talk of this kid who played a joke on this nutty teacher years ago.

This kid in decades to pass probably would not enjoy particular fame. Maybe she would be a mom herself, quiet and unappreciated. This person as an adult would have never imagined that that day in crazy Mrs. McKinney's class would be not only her time in the limelight, but her swan song because nothing that grandiose would ever happen to her again.

Ceci wished she were the Holden Caulfield of these moments. She wanted to be like Holden from *The Catcher in the Rye* who pictured himself as the savior of numerous children running and playing in a huge rye field on the edge of a precipice. His job was to catch the children if they wandered too close to the brink. Holden thought he was alluding to a phrase in Burns' "comin' through the rye." Ceci would never have gotten that wrong. When a body sees a body, coming through the rye. Did it really matter that that crazy kid got the words to the poem wrong? Did it matter?

Does anything I do really matter, Ceci thought.

It was a beautiful moment when a bunch of kids conspired to tease a teacher and put up a quiet kid whom the teacher would not suspect would pull a joke on her or on anyone. Would they know that joke would be one of the sweetest things anyone would ever do for that kid?

Allison couldn't thank the class; they wouldn't care for a thank you or need it. All they wanted was to fool Ceci, Ceci to be surprised and then pretend she was angry. She did everything they wanted. And all were satisfied.

And Allison was happy she didn't have to raise her hand anymore.

Chapter 38

She took the phone call in the principal's office.

"Uh huh. Uh huh. Okay. No, I will be there after school. What time do they close? All right. Works out fine, then. See you later. Toodles."

Neil Jackson knew what the phone call was about.

"Ceci, only one period left. Naomi can cover for you. You should go home," he said.

"And let that...thing...teach one of my classes? Oh no, no, no. I'll leave the regular time. Don't worry, the place won't close. It's just a business—a dying business—but a business." She waited for Neil to react, but he didn't.

The period went surprisingly fast and she felt inexplicably good. See, she thought, the world was not coming apart. There were no collisions, no meteors crashing, Haley's comet was not due and there was just a calm. Granted, it did seem unnatural, but she could get used to anything.

She was empty and she was full; she was tired and she was energetic; she was in great humor and she was morose. It was a typical Ceci day. She reflected on the phone call and forgot who had called her. She had an idea, but she couldn't be sure.

She decided to lock her classroom door, something she hadn't done in thirty years of teaching. She signed out, something she also never did, except when a strike date was set and the teachers were strongly advised to by the Union. Chairpersons didn't engage in the Union-backed tactics regular classroom teachers did, but Ceci loved the fight, for whatever side. She would always be a teacher, she proudly proclaimed. The administration tolerated her; the teachers loved her for it.

Because they all knew where her heart lay, she could tell her department members anything, give them any directive and they would follow it blindly. She was that good. Signing out was a new experience for her. When she did sign out, the teachers who were standing in line let her get in front of them.

She got into her white Infiniti G35 sport with the racing car spoiler. She could hear Jaime commenting, "Your car is *so* not mother-ish. Did you need red leather interior? It really is too cool for you, Mom. That should belong to me."

She drove for about a mile and pulled over to the shoulder of Sunrise Highway and decided to put her head back and close her eyes for five minutes. When she opened her eyes, she was amazed at how pitch it had gotten.

"Wow," she said aloud.

"It's so dark at 3:30. Maybe a storm is approaching and we are in its eye. If I'm in it, it's a black eye."

Her watch must have broken because it showed 10:30.

"It's what you get from buying cheap batteries in a thrift store. Got to go to the jeweler in town tomorrow." She eased back onto the highway and headed home, just 20 minutes away.

"Da mudder's home," she announced. "Where's the fodder?" She always loved to say that mudder ate fodder. "The mudder wants the fodder."

Damn, it was taking her forever to get to the couch and how loud her footsteps were. She took off her jacket, dropped her briefcase and plopped onto the recliner.

"Babe," Tim whispered. "I've been so worried. Why don't you put your jacket back on, okay?"

"Fodder, mudder just took her riding blanket off. You don't re-blanket a mudder right away and certainly fodder doesn't talk."

"Let me help you," he said and draped it over her; Jaime and Jimmy stayed behind watching.

"Clean up those stalls," they heard her say. "Don't force me to summon Hercules. Remember the Twelve Labors of Hercules? The fifth labor, the Augean Stables? Oh sure you do, my pretties. He can do it you know. Very easy for him. Swoosh, and voilá all the hay and poop would become part of the Alpheus River. I just love a guy with muscles."

"Everything will be done Mom when you come home. Promise," said Jaime who rarely did house chores.

"Are you getting cute with me, young lady," Ceci said pretty sure Jaime was up to something. She was never indulgent, least of all to Ceci.

"Promise, Mommy," Jaime said. Ceci could swear Jaime's voice sounded different, but she doubted it as Jaime rarely showed emotion or affection for Ceci. She looked up at Jimmy who just gave her a thumbs up and turned around.

"Nice, horsy," she said to Tim stroking his soft red mane, "and what does my stud say? Do you now see why I should have married a good old Italian boy? You would have been my Italian stallion. But, noo, you had to be Irish. My mother was right." Tim put his arm around his wife.

Tim and Ceci needed to go to the funeral home.

"Now how the hell am I going to pick out a dress for my mother? She is such a pain in the butt. I'll be hearing the complaints for the rest of my life. Anyway, it's too damn late."

"They understand and said they'll reopen for us later tonight," Tim said.

"No, it's off to Friendly Friendly's Funeral Fantasyland first. By the way, young stallion, this is totally distasteful to me."

"I know it is, but we have to identify the body first. The funeral home is after."

"My mother knows who she is," she yelled.

"I'll drive," he said, leading her out of the living room.

"Are you sure you have your learner's permit. This is a job for grown-ups." He just sighed and would have shaken his head if he didn't know how hard this was going to be.

She wanted to go to the funeral home to pick out a lavender dress. Somehow doing that first would have prolonged the life of Gilda. For that 25-minute detour, Gilda would have still been alive to Ceci since she would not have identified the body yet.

Chapter 39

For some reason, the living room had gotten so small she could not stand up in it, let alone walk to the door. What happened to it? She didn't remember her house ever being that tiny. Sure, she told Tim regularly that he had to *do* something, anything. She wanted her home expanded, but was never very specific as to what she wanted done. Tim believed she was complaining about nothing that was pressing. She associated her dissatisfaction with her life with the appearance of her house. He could do much with the house, but fixing Ceci would take some doing.

This time, she felt constricted like the time she and Tim were in Venice a year ago during Lent and the festival of the *Carnivale*. The crowds customarily funneled into the walkways which normally accommodated three walkers abreast between the rows of boutiques and bistros. It was doable as the walk was not too long and one could slip into a shop to browse to avoid the daily crowds. That day Ceci was struck by a panic only Tim could handle for her. The crowds of vacationers rushing to reach Saint Mark's Square were at least ten abreast which forced people to maintain a brisk pace and didn't allow for anyone to stop or even hesitate a bit. She felt herself being strangled. Shop owners locked their doors to browsers. Only serious shoppers intending to purchase were considered entry. Using a restroom was forbidden without a sizeable store purchase. When she realized she was trapped in a barely-moving crowd and had no control over her walking, Tim saw and felt her fear. He held her hands above her and they both awkwardly kept pace with the others.

"Look up," he said. "Do you think it will rain?" For the few seconds she thought of the weather, she felt safe. Tim spoke and Ceci saw his lips move. More seconds passed. It was just enough time to reach the square and follow the crowd waiting for a water taxi to take them away from St. Mark's. Tim held her until her trembling stopped. She loved Venice too much to hate that day. And she loved Tim too much that day.

"Let's go straight to our hotel, okay?" she said.

"Don't you want to stop off at Murano? You like those glasses."

"I don't think I can do it, Tim."

Why was this damn room getting smaller and smaller, Ceci thought. It was going to crush her. That was what it always felt like when Gilda fought with Ceci; when Gilda lectured Ceci; when Gilda would not go home. Oh, she would think, my life would be so uncomplicated if that woman died. My life would be easy. I am so sick of her and her antics, really.

Ceci did not remember, but she must have identified the body; she must have picked out a dress from the funeral home. She must have because it was the next day.

"We have to get going, Hon," said Tim.

"Get going where, for goodness sake?" Ceci asked. Sometimes Tim made no sense at all. She picked off some of Goldie's white dog hair from his dark blue suit and adjusted his black mourning tie. She checked the room to make sure Jaime was wearing all black and hadn't sneaked in a vivid multi-colored something and that Jimmy had on a black tie, as well.

"Okay," she sang, everybody in the car. We are going to a pah-tee."

Jaime and Jimmy each cupped one of Ceci's elbows. She wriggled out of Jaime's hold and let Jimmy lead her. Not reacting to the snub, Jaime made sure her mother was seated in the Infiniti and buckled in.

"Afraid your old lady is going to fall out? Too late," said Ceci.

Jimmy shook his head as he looked at Jaime. Helping her into the back seat, he squeezed his sister's trembling hand.

They entered the Antonio Funeral Home and tried to guide Ceci in. She stiffened and refused their help.

"I do not need anybody to show me how to walk, damn it." What on earth had come over them, she thought. Haven't they ever gone to a party?

"Doesn't the hostess look pretty in that lavender dress. The veil over her shoulders is quite stunning. She really is being rude, though, by reposing, instead of greeting her guests."

Tim put his arm around Ceci's waist.

"Ya know, Tim, I don't think I want to stay if she is not going to be a vivacious hostess."

Ceci was about to awaken the hostess to chat when she realized her own legs could not support her weight. As a matter of fact, none of her family could support them, either.

"Alan, damn you. Where are you? Don't tell me you're sleeping, too?"

Tim was a bigger and taller man than Alan was, but only Alan would have been able to hold her up. Tim felt he had supported her for many years, but Ceci didn't think so. Even Alan would have felt confident that Tim could hold her up, but her brother wasn't always right. And Alan wasn't there.

Ceci was very confused. Why was the air so heavy to breathe? Who decorated this dreary place? Miss Havisham? And what was Gilda doing in a coffin in a funeral home?

She took a closer look at the hostess' dress and said, "Who selected that hideous outfit? Definitely not something my mother would have picked."

She heard someone wailing. Damn how annoying that was when she was trying to concentrate.

"Come on, Mom, try to stand up. Let me help you," said Jimmy.

Would that moron please stop screaming, she thought. She wiped her hands onto her slacks and was glad she was dressed all in black. None of the blood would show.

"Come on, Mommy," Jimmy said, his voice cracking. Jaime also helped lift Ceci and she could now easily be walked to an armchair of the first row in front of Gilda's coffin.

What on earth was Ceci doing in this room and how she hated the smell of gladioli. Even the red rosebud rosary beads draped over the tufted velvet coffin cover liner stank.

Chapter 40

Ceci didn't argue too much when Neil Jackson suggested she take the rest of the school year off. She had enough accumulated days in her sick bank to cover the time and her retirement incentive would fall into place nicely. She said she would think about it.

Each day followed the next and the next and was as lifeless as the one before. The decision had to be made and Tim was not up to it. The children tried to make it a shared decision, but Tim refused their help.

"We can't let her live like this," Jaime started. "Dad, do something. You have to."

"We can't jump the gun," he said. "This is very delicate."

"She is vegetating. She doesn't do anything. No medicine. No food. Nothing. Do you want her to…"

"Don't! You don't have the luxury, young lady, or permission to say one word about your mother."

Jaime exhaled loudly and marched out of the living room. She looked at Jimmy who refused to say anything. He couldn't. He didn't know what to say.

"And then what?" Jaime said from the next room, "maybe stick tubes into her?"

"If we have to until she gets better, yeah."

"And if she doesn't *want* to get better, huh, Dad?"

Tim ultimately relented and allowed the hospital to send an ambulance and take Ceci away. To avoid being restrained, she didn't fight and settled herself into the coffin-like stretcher. Jaime cried and Jimmy vomited and vomited.

Clinical depression. Nervous breakdown. Bipolar disorder. Other people suffered these, not Ceci. She refused to assign any of her feelings of sadness, of confusion, of anger to the death of Gilda. Didn't she always say her life would be better without Gilda in it to destroy it little by little? She wasn't going to miss Gilda. She was Ceci. She would figure out a way where she wouldn't be able to think about anything. She would find a way out.

She knew what she needed, not these people pretending to be doctors and therapists and who were sure they knew what was good for her. It was a typical case of teacher burnout she told the doctors.

She was resistant to group therapy and caused much animosity among the other patients. Whether she agreed or not, individual therapy did help her as the doctors were more apt to be accepting of her sarcasm because of Tim.

Two months passed and Ceci regained her strength. Physically, she was strong. Emotionally? Everyone hoped so. Tim was sure Ceci knew what she was doing. She always did.

It was she, not he, who was in control. He had to stay strong for the kids even though they were solid kids and could handle themselves. Sometimes it seemed like they were handling him.

Time passed and the doctors saw no reason why Ceci couldn't be released to Tim with the promise that she would get therapy on an out-patient basis for an extended period.

Tim had finished cooking and called all to the table.

"How utterly unoriginal, yet very American of you," Ceci said as Tim served up the hamburgers and hot dogs. "You do realize that these are really German things. Hamburg, Germany and Frankfurt, Germany. Any reason you are serving German disguised as American?"

Ceci looked as though she was trying to be witty, but Tim was not sure. Either her jokes were weak or Tim was too weak to laugh. In either event, Ceci was home.

She would be going back to work soon and Tim and Neil, the principal, were concerned.

Chapter 41

Whenever Ceci taught mythology, she always began with the same lesson and proceeded the same way. She'd turn off the classroom lights and close the blinds. The kids relished whatever was going to happen.

"Lights out. Cool."

"Okay, now. I want you to close your eyes."

The students would have done anything to please Ceci and enjoy a respite from the typical class lesson of taking out homework, groaning at what the homework assignment for the night was, learning that there would be a quiz tomorrow and please turn around and spit out the gum.

"No, no. Don't spit it into my pail. Do you do that at home?" she'd ask and then fearing their answer added, "Well you can't do that here. Put it in a piece of paper first. No, don't take a sheet of my Shakespeare pad." She loved those octagonal sheets that fit into the cardboard replica of the Globe Theater. The plume pen had been stolen the first day. The pad had been a gift from her good friend Sonia. She liked the pad because she liked Sonia.

"Try to imagine what life was like as far back in time as you could go." Ceci would wait the few seconds the kids could wait without getting impatient. If the wait time was too long, they'd open their eyes, look at anyone else around them, and ruin the mood by giggling.

"Are you there, yet?" she'd continue. "Good. Now go a little further back." She knew she had them and she loved it. When they opened their eyes, she would be at the board and she would write "Chaos."

"At that time that you can imagine, long, long ago, there was earth, water and dirt swirling, blowing around, and around and crashing into each other, creating…" and she'd point to the title she had written on the board.

With Ceci dramatic flair, she'd run to the board and underline with her finger "Chaos." How she loved when she knew she had hooked the group. They stared and waited for more.

"And out of this chaos came a kind of order…" and she would begin charting a family tree for her Greek mythology lesson.

"There was Gaea, Uranus, the titans." Then she got to the good stuff, the gods and goddesses and their realms of power.

"Cronus, god of time, Zeus, the king of the gods. Hera, queen of the gods. By the way, Hera was Zeus' wife and also his sister." She waited for their oohs, yucks, and icks.

"Geez, I wouldn't marry *my* sister!" somebody would always say.

"Neither would I," somebody would answer and the class, including Ceci, would hoot.

"Aphrodite, goddess of love, beauty and sexuality. Some scholars believe that Cronus castrated Uranus and threw his genitals into the sea. Aphrodite was born of the sea foam caused by the discarded genitals."

The boys laughed as the girls tittered. Ceci took pleasure in the students' reactions and how involved they were becoming.

"We have Athena, goddess of wisdom, who was born from the brain of Zeus."

She loved mythology because she found it very easy to believe. Yes, the immortals suffered, but it was noble suffering. Yes, there was chaos, but there was an explanation for it. She felt that world welcomed her just the way she was, Olympian warts and all.

It had always been difficult for her to break away from the worlds other writers created. Until now, she merely presented these worlds and characters and she would live in these settings with her students for 42 minutes at a time. She was comfortable there and she was having a harder and harder time returning.

"What am I doing here?" she said. She looked around the room—at the kids, at the posters, at the windows, at the floor. "What am I *doing* here?" She excused herself, left the room and walked the halls. She could hear the class begin to talk nervously among themselves.

"What the hell just happened?"

"Where'd she go? Shhh. She's liable to walk in any minute."

But Ceci didn't, not in the next ten minutes or for the next thirty minutes. The bell rang signalling the end of the period and the kids went to their next class still buzzing about what Mrs. McKinney did.

"Don't care..." said Ryan. "We had a free period."

"Yeah, I texted my boyfriend in peace," said Dana, "without her telling me to hand over my phone."

"Think she'll be absent from class next period?"

Ceci checked her mail, saw that nobody gave a damn to leave a message and she disregarded the typical school memos she rarely read anyway. It was those hideous pink sheets she would glance at. Not necessarily heed, but nevertheless she would glance at them. It was 11:20 and Louise presumed Ceci was going to her car to get the lunch she had forgotten there as she had done so often of late.

"That brainless dodo would forget her head if it weren't attached," said Louise.

Oh, she remembered her head. Unfortunately, her head was swirling around with Gaea and Uranus with interruptions by Cronus who had a time thing. Time to get out of her head. Time to get out of this damn building. Time to wonder where on earth she was going. But going she was and fast. She started the car and was out of the parking lot faster than those colleagues who sneaked out of the building before the final bell.

The gods and goddesses were chasing her—or were they helping her move fast, fast, fast. She loved those deities because they kept her company for her entire career. She was all of them. She was Athena and came from Zeus' brain. She was Hercules and could complete those twelve labors faster than he ever could. She was Demeter and didn't have to bargain with her brother Hades to get her daughter Persephone out of the underworld. She knew what it was like to walk the Halls of Hades and it wasn't all that scary. And, unlike, Eurydice, she could leave any damn time she wanted with impunity.

Look back? If she wanted to. Get out okay? If she chose to. She always thought Orpheus didn't turn back because he was a wimp. Alan would have. She was Aphrodite; she was Apollo and his twin sister Artemis. And all the stories were about her. It was mythology, she'd tell her students when they'd question the illogic in some of the stories.

"Mythology," she'd say. "Fake stories. Not true."

Ah, but they *were* true.

Ceci was becoming everything and everybody she taught. She assumed the personalities of all the characters. She was the character and characteristics of every student she had. She inhaled everything and became everything.

She wondered as she was driving away from work, where was Ceci? Was there any kind of metaphysical exchange of some sort? When she took on all these people, did they in turn become Ceci? What a ghastly thought.

She tried to imagine a world with billions of Cecis. All totally nuts. All needy. All sad excuses for humanity. All having a Gilda for a mother. Yikes, billions of Gildas. The entire cosmic order would surely be affected, disintegrated by

Gildas. Billions of Jaimes. Billions of Jimmys—which was okay by her.

And then there would be billions of Tims. All silent. All allowing those billions of Cecis to do what they wanted, but all Holden Caulfields preventing them from running off the cliff, saving them all from running through the rye and falling off billions of cliffs.

Chapter 42

Ceci pulled into a Seven-11 after driving nowhere in particular for two and a half hours. She was tired. She hated those long driving hauls. Damn. She probably needed gas. She could count on Tim to fill up her tank. She checked the gas gauge and noticed she still had half a tank. Was it normal for a husband to make sure his wife's tank was full? Did all husbands do that? Or did husbands with wives like Ceci only do that? Billions of husbands can't be wrong.

She didn't remember the last time she was so tired. She really needed to see a therapist for the pronounced slur in her speech. Come to think of it, she should see an orthopedist about her limping. She needed to see a circus performer to see if her finger dexterity to thread pens through her fingers was as good as Neil Jackson's. She would have to see a neurologist to find out why sometimes she could only move one hand and the other three appendages were useless and lifeless. What the hell happened to her vocal chords? Grunting her way through life would be totally unacceptable.

Sitting in the car, she leaned her head over and came to attention to see who was ringing his damn horn. Non-stop.

She leaned back to check and the ringing stopped. She rested her forehead onto her opened palm and stayed that way until the sweat started to annoy her. Wiping her palms onto her jacket and then dusting off the lint that stuck to her hand, flicking here and there, she slid out of the car.

She looked at the large banner over the green and red Seven-11 logo.

"Good. I'm starved." Wonder what they sell in this store. Never been here before." She decided to window shop. Surely something would be in the store she could eat. The cashier greeted her.

"Hi, Mrs. McKinney."

"Yes, I must know you, dear," she said. The cashier laughed and told Ceci she was a rip. She asked Ceci if she was playing hooky and Ceci thought the cashier was trying to make a joke and laughed to make her feel better.

What in hell is she talking about, she wondered but kept that question to herself. She was everybody today and it would be very difficult to sort them all out and file all the information. The processing would be much too time consuming. Then she would have to consult Cronus.

She figured out what to buy.

"Coffee and a corn dog." She paid, winked at the cashier and left. She didn't know what time it was and wondered if she should be hungry at that time.

Oh, great, she thought. Her car had a clock and a clock would tell her what time it was. She noticed the time and wondered what connection it had to do with whatever she was doing. Was she doing anything? Was she supposed to be doing something? For a minute she forgot what car she had been driving.

It was lucky for her that she noticed a car with its door flung open and the engine still running. Nobody better have bumped into the door because then she could sue. She never sued anybody in her life and really didn't know how one went about it. Tim's brother was an attorney, so she felt empowered.

Fortunately, the car was in park. If she had put it in drive, would it drive itself?

"What a wonderful concept," she said. "Airplanes fly on their own. Why can't my car?"

She was ecstatic to learn that she did indeed have a car that could drive itself. She put the gear in drive because it was obvious that this damn machine wasn't going to even try to be progressive and put itself in gear. She tried to tell it that one has to depress the accelerator for it to do anything.

"Okay, okay," she said. "I will help you, you ignorant machine, but then you are on your own." She was going to enjoy the jaunt. She accelerated as far as her foot could go and left the automatic pilot to tend to the Infiniti.

She slid over to the passenger seat and rested her head for a moment.

And then everything got dark.

Chapter 43

It was either Jaime or Jimmy who spoke.

"Mom?"

Wow, what a trip, thought Ceci. Windows flying past. White sheets blowing about her. Gurney wheels bumping over polished black and white diamond-patterned ceramic tiles. Glaring recessed lighting checkerboarding the pimpled ceiling tiles. Machines blipped and pinged with their blinking red lights and squiggly lines. Plastic tubing coming out from bodies. Movement. Dollied as a shipment from a home improvement store.

Somebody was examining her head. On the outside? On the inside? Take it easy. Need this stuff to improve the house. Got to make the living quarters accessible to any professional who desired to enter. Got to make it appear better even though it might have Poe's House of Usher crack in it.

Madeline and Roderick Usher lived together. Or was it just Roderick? That house was at one time a sign of complete Usher opulence. It must have been the symbol of strength, completeness. Eventually, like Ceci, the outward appearance did have signs of a crack splitting the entire structure.

The iceberg effect? What do they say about icebergs being only 10% above the surface with the bulk of its strength and appearance hidden below the surface? Is it really hidden? Perhaps for the unsuspecting birds, the Jonathan Seagulls flying above it, but not to the sea life swimming around it to avoid collision. It is also visible to anyone or anything that *cares* to submerge.

One has to dare to submerge oneself. Then what? All the deep sea, scuba equipment in the world cannot prepare a diver for the scope and breadth of the enormity of that iceberg. Can the diver bore through it so he can swim through? Build a kind of tunnel? If someone could come up with a good reason, would he build that tunnel? It was so much easier to simply avoid the iceberg and spend the extra time swimming or deep sea traveling around it. The braver guides or seamen could travel very close to it if they were willing to risk touching it.

"Mom," and the voice seemed to be getting louder, almost to the point of irritation. The owner of that questioning voice was very vague. The person behind that voice had a face and a body, but Ceci wondered why the person deliberately blurred herself. She knew it was a girl. The word of question, Mom, was getting more high pitched. The question mark seemed clearer with each raising of the octave.

The only way for that piercing interruption to the quiet, comforting droning around her to be silenced was to respond to it.

"Hey," was all Ceci could manage.

"Mommy, Mommy," Jaime said, her voice sounding juvenile between the jerked sobs a child makes when she has not been granted whatever it was she had been wanting for so long.

"Ouch," and a moan was all that Ceci could muster. Jaime's squeezing and attempt at lifting Ceci from the bed to hug her was painful. For the first time in a long time, it was not painful for Jaime to hug her mother. Not the way it was for Ceci to hug Gilda. But Jaime was lucky. Ceci hadn't been allowed to hug Gilda. She was stopped by the funeral director and by Tim. Why couldn't she lift her mother from her coffin to hug her. Why? Those idiots and everyone else around her, namely Jaime and Jimmy, just didn't know that she wanted to hug her damn mother. And this time Gilda wouldn't be able to object with simply patting Ceci on the back as was her way of hugging her daughter back.

Ceci swore she would never discourage a hug from her children, so when Jaime tried, Ceci wanted to stifle the moan, but couldn't. Everything hurt too much.

"What happened?" Ceci asked any who was present— husband, children or doctor.

"A little fender bender," Dr. Thomas said.

"Ah, I see," said Ceci, trying not to move too much. "Do any fenders work?"

"Yours do, but I don't know about the car's," Tim offered. Timmy was being funny, she sang to herself. She had fractured her nose, clavicle and both shoulders. One wrist was broken and she had three bruised ribs.

"The sodium azide releasing the nitrogen gas as the airbag deployed caused extensive burns to your face and forehead," the doctor said. "The discomfort you feel when you breathe is nothing compared to what could have happened if that air bad didn't deploy."

"Could just see the headlines: Head Challenges Windshield—Windshield Wins," Ceci said. Tim bent down and lightly kissed her forehead.

The time of convalescence went directly into retirement and Ceci had plenty of time to reflect. She thought of Alan and whenever she did, everything felt good. There was always that feeling of tepid water drizzling all over her. She didn't open her mouth to drink the water; feeling it was much better than imbibing it. Drinking tepid water made her gag. Why was that, she often wondered. Was the purpose of tasteless liquid merely to become part of her inner body temperature and nothing else? Soup was either warm or hot and it was pleasant. She guessed because it did have some taste before it became part of her.

Her brother Alan was an extension of her own body. Every time she read Poe's "The Fall of the House of Usher," she felt a kinship. She and Alan were kind of like Madeline and Roderick Usher growing up in a house with a crack going down the middle.

Chapter 44

Sometimes she was not in the hospital, but back at school. She'd better make up her mind, she thought, as to where she chose to be. *She* decided where she would be, not her mind.

Today she was back at Alcmene. Period seven was always dreaded by the math section on the second floor. That was the period that Blanche had what she called her only "bad" class. All of Blanche's classes were unmanageable to her, yet they were controllable to other teachers. Her class was right above Ceci's and she was fighting her impulse to storm upstairs and knock the students' heads together while pushing Blanche's face in.

Blanche suffered from a form of narcolepsy and would fall asleep in class. All teachers at one point in their lives dozed off while the students were reading aloud, especially if they were reading round-robin. It was a clever way to catch up on one's sleep provided the teacher was seated in the back of the room. The kids had to be cooperative and aware enough to know when two paragraphs were finished. The students, if savvy enough, could gauge when their turn would come, hence guaranteeing more than one person could nap at the same time. That worked fine and nobody complained. It always amazed Ceci at how they could sense when it was their turn to read and awaken and continue at the precise spot. If ever someone began a paragraph that had been read aloud already, the complaints of the kids who actually may have liked the story caused the rest to be more diligent and attentive. In either event, Ceci always managed to steal a few winks.

Nobody could nod off in class when Blanche was teaching seventh period. Tired that her students needed to move their desks close to each other in order to hear what everybody was saying, Ceci decided to solve the problem. Laden with tennis balls and a box cutter, she went upstairs to Blanche's room. When Ceci entered the classroom, the kids were delighted at both seeing their English teacher, as well as wondering why she brought up 100 tennis balls. She sat at a desk and motioned to a few of the students to hand the balls to her when she was finished cutting a cross into each. Blanche was very confused, more of the quiet of the class than at Ceci cutting into tennis balls.

"Now, everybody turn your desks upside down" Ceci ordered. Clanging and dragging and crashing was sure to anger all those teachers on the first floor if it hadn't been for Ceci's asking them all to indulge her for the beginning of period 7. She assured those teachers that she was going to resolve all their problems. They wouldn't be sorry as long as they could bear a little extra noise coming from Blanche's room. They couldn't imagine how that phenomenon could be possible. Every one of Blanche's classes was noisy.

"Each one of you is to come here and bring four tennis balls." The kids understood what she wanted to do and each put a ball with the cross cuts onto each of the metal chair legs. They flipped the desks over and voilá, only the silent, smooth velvety dragging sound could be heard from school tennis ball-shod chairs.

Now all the teachers, especially Ceci, had to put up with the loudness of the students and not the dragging, screeching of the desks, as well. One only worried if the class was too silent. That could only mean that Blanche had fallen completely asleep and the class was wandering the halls. Ceci was impressed at how quietly—so opposite to the way they entered math class—they could sneak out of the class and how gingerly they could descend the stairs. And no one had a pass. Sometimes, they had a pass from the day earlier. The hall monitors rarely checked closely for the handwritten date. The kids would flash the yellow Alcmene hall pass, acknowledge the lady and say a few pleasant words. Few kids were polite to the hall monitors and out of gratitude for being treated kindly, the monitors simply smiled back and waved them on. The kids knew how to disperse and take different staircases—those roads all leading to the same Rome—the cafeteria and the snack machines.

Chapter 45

L ying in the hospital bed, Ceci tried to fill in a lot of missing sections in her brain. Tim, Jaime and Jimmy agreed to leave, but promised to return for the evening visiting hours. She was relieved because she had a lot of work to do, a lot of unaccounted hours to reconcile. She became frustrated that nothing was making sense. That's always the way her dreams were.

Ceci envied people who had normal dreams. Occasionally, she would have one of a past boyfriend who came back and while on a very romantic date, he would try to kiss her and after some dainty refusals, she would kiss him back. And then she would wake up sorry she had to kiss Tim good morning. This guy in the dream did not have morning breath. It was in the afternoon and in a dream, she'd tell herself. Give Tim a break for God's sake. Others would relate their dreams of winning the lottery and moving to a deserted island with Hollywood's sexiest. That was a dream she would gladly make up, only her dreams were usually disjointed.

A typical dream would be Ceci talking to Alan who was dead, but he wasn't. Her father Gino would walk in, who was dead, but wasn't. Joining them would be some of her students, only Marshall walked and spoke eloquently. No one in the dream commented on how beautiful he was, and Ceci would have to point it out to them. They would laugh at her and ask Clarence Gummajian, now not needing to play the role of Ceci in front of a class. He was Ceci holding the classroom erasers while passing out Combos. Or Ceci would be in her nightgown and realize it when she started her lesson. She needed her coat, but she had to walk past the class to get to her office in the back of the room. She always left her coat thrown over a chair. This time the coat was locked in her wardrobe closet and the key was melting in one of Salvador Dali's paintings.

As soon as she woke up, she would try to go back to sleep and adjust the dream, removing the parts she didn't approve of. She would leave in Alan and Gino, but that never worked because she could never get back into that dream because she knew it was contrived. It was just like when she awoke from a pleasant dream and wanted to quickly go back to it to prolong the ecstasy at seeing her brother and father again. She really didn't need those dreams because she always daydreamed about each of them, anyway.

Then she was Oedipus wanting his mother. Then she was Electra wanting her father. She could really give Freud a run for his mother, that's for sure. She didn't have the luxury of time and money to talk to a psychiatrist.

Not until now.

She remembered having to teach a lesson in mythology, but couldn't get Marshall out of her mind. She was feeling exceptionally depressed at the life—whatever the quality of it was—that this child had to live. To succumb to? His world was as silent as she sometimes wanted hers to be. Lately, she needed it to be like that more and more. She wondered where he went when he got distracted. Did he daydream? Did he think of things? Was there sound? How would he snap out of it? No noise would jog him. The nudge of his chair wheels by his teacher aid Stephanie might do it; a light tap on his chest might do it. It didn't matter if you playfully kicked his lifeless legs and that thought saddened Ceci.

Glimpses of memory frames would appear, but not remain long enough for her to splice anything coherent together. She needed to fill in the empty slots of her recall. Thoughts of Marshall dominated as she tried to prepare for her mythology lesson.

She had had a plan. Some day soon she would tell his signer Tracy and aid Stephanie to leave Marshall.

"Don't worry. I can handle him. And leave his book bag," she'd say. They looked at each other.

Tracy would say, "Okay. It would be nice having a few minutes alone. Maybe even chat with some of the other kids without our boy here demanding to know what we're saying."

"Great," Ceci would say. "Got a few strategies I want to try on him."

She had been teaching herself how to mindspeak and she would experiment with Marshall. It might work, but first things first. She would close the door and wheel him into her office.

Ceci was sweating and asked the nurse if she could turn up the air conditioning. The nurse removed some of Ceci's blankets and assured her that she would feel better soon as the thermostats were set automatically and all the rooms on that floor needed to stay at the proscribed temperature.

"Hospital orders, you know," said the nurse. Her even expression connoted authority and Ceci could hear "not a chance, kiddo."

This was the precise spot in her recollection that was giving her so much trouble. She couldn't fill in some of the events at this point. No matter, she thought, it would all come back to her. She remembered some more and it was a pleasant memory.

She was finally going to test her mindspeaking. She would think what she wanted to say to Marshall and he, in his special way, would be able to hear her and mindspeak back. To her delight it was working and he was responding to exactly what she was saying and what was more astonishing and pleasing to her, he was responding with exactly *what* she wanted him to say. This, she thought, had to be the highpoint of her existence. She found a way to give this damaged child some peace, some freedom. His mindspeech would free him and would feed her. This exchange of food, this intellectual repast, thrilled her.

Then she was back in her car and was speeding on to find the nearest Seven-11. There it goes again, she thought. My kind of dreaming. I am going to Seven-11 and I am lying in a hospital bed. I can do it, she thought. This is the way I live.

And she forgot all about Marshall. She forgot about the gods and goddesses. Jesus would be her sub for the day. He was good that way. She wondered, though, if He were certified to teach English. The administration was a real stickler for things like that.

And she fell asleep.

Chapter 46

She didn't know if she were sleeping or talking with someone. She knew she was a child and was different from other children. Other kids did not have Gilda for a mother. Other kids did not have Gino for a dad—and she felt sorry for them—and other kids did not have Alan to protect them every damned day of their lives. Although Ceci didn't appreciate him then, she did now. Didn't that count for something?

Gilda fawned over Alan every chance she got. Gino always believed Alan could change the world. In truth, he could only affect the outcome of Ceci's world if he wanted to. Gino could also, but he had Gilda to put up with. His affections to Ceci were limited to when the time was right—when Gilda was not within hearing or seeing.

Ceci knew the rules. She would wait until Gilda was not around and then snuggle up to Gino. He never refused and he always managed to give her side winks and smiles whenever Gilda turned her head. Those piecemeal moments of attention sufficed for the child. She could count the times Gilda paid extra mind to her. Why, then, did some of her friends always say that Gilda slobbered over her. Ceci didn't remember that.

When she became an adult, Gilda was relentless in her criticizing of Ceci which she accepted because she felt she deserved it.

Ceci wondered if she were awake because she was aware of a kind of clarity for what she craved: quiet. Only Marshall had quiet within him, around him and directed to him. Only Marshall really knew what was happening in life. Only Marshall's world had the calm and gentility and innocence Ceci craved. No smart alecky people. Nobody enjoying to see her squirm. Nobody insulting her and telling her she didn't know how to raise kids. No students who really didn't care if they learned or not. No administrators who questioned the veracity of her thoughts, the professional judgment calls. No department members who laughed behind her back and were sure they could do a better job.

Marshall's was a world she wanted to be in. She knew if she approached Marshall, he would let her see what it was like. Getting into his world was not going to be an easy task. With any other students, you simply asked about their lives and then gradually without their being aware of it you could start probing, probing, into what their worlds were like. You could have after-school meetings and talk to them. You could talk until you saw something about them you liked or wanted and then you simply assumed those characteristics.

It was easy enough to limp; it was easy enough to stutter, why even threading a pen through your fingers was not that hard. It didn't get you far, though, because then your husband would stare at you. Your kids would stare at you.

Staring would not get an invitation into her world.

Negotiating into Marshall's world would have to be much more orchestrated so that even he wouldn't know he was inviting you in. Ceci couldn't afford to be disappointed.

She definitely was awake, but she was also very tired. How could anyone be expected to remember every second of the day? Why, she couldn't remember what she had for breakfast, as they said. Ceci *really* couldn't remember.

Her forehead was itchy. It hurt when she tried to scratch it. She didn't know if it were the sensitivity of her burned skin or the sensitivity of her injured hand. In each case, an itch had to be scratched. And by golly, it was going to be scratched.

"Mrs. McKinney, what are you doing, dear," said the nurse. Ceci hated being called *dear*. She was not this Nurse Ratched's dear and she didn't want to be, either.

She wished she wanted to be Tim's dear. She had been at one time, but she didn't think so anymore. She didn't deserve to be. She could be an ogress, but that is what she liked about herself. She liked acting the shrew, Shakespeare's Katharina, but Tim was not Petruchio and did not know how to tame her. Using Petruchio's reverse psychology of telling Katharina that she was "pleasant, gamesome, and passing courteous" would never, never work on Ceci. Sometimes she wanted to be pampered; sometimes she didn't. He was supposed to know when to do which.

And he used to, but now he was wearing down. The hospital suggested Tim work from home, to record what was necessary so he could see and observe more. It would make the proposed therapy more effective. After all, he was not administrator of the Center. He was only assistant in charge. Tim would run the Center when Noel Christian was out.

"Does Noel know they are paying you to stay home and work and you are really not doing your job?"

"Why do you say that, Cee?"

"You are supposed to be observing. Where's your freaking clipboard like the real doctors? Timothy McKinney, you are a failure. And you don't have Ceci to wipe up after you."

"Mrs. McKinney," the nurse repeated, not angrily, but determined to either get an answer from Ceci or get her to desist from rubbing her forehead.

"Do you have a headache?"

"I have an itch," Ceci said trying to be calm at the ridiculousness of the question. "When one has an itch, one scratches it. Correct? And surely you know what it's like to be an itch, don't you?"

The nurse smiled and dampened a cloth and wiped Ceci's forehead. Then she tore open a little packet of an antiseptic pad and wiped the blood that had gathered from the scratching. Until the alcohol dried, the slicing burning made Ceci wince. The wincing, in turn, caused the tenderness to pinch even more.

"Is there anything I can get you, Mrs. McKinney?"

"Uh, some understanding, perhaps. I know, I know. Only what's on the shelves."

Ceci kind of hoped to get a confrontational smile from Nurse Ratched. She needed someone to blame her predicament of broken bones, sore, very sore ribs, and aching forehead.

It was difficult to think. And would no one help her think? Then again, she didn't want anyone to help her think and she got annoyed whenever anyone questioned her about anything. What a nasty world. Good thing she was going to see what Marshall's world was like, even if she had to force him to take her along.

"Well, good morning, Mrs. McKinney," said Noel Christian. "Did you sleep well? What happened to your head?"

"Is that a loaded question, Dr. Christian, or do you make it a habit of not reading the patient chart? One's whole life charted out to the way the patient wants it to look or is it the way the charter sees it? If the chartee is a bitch, do the entries change? Do they get doctored?"

"Boo, you can do better than that, Ceci," he said. "What the hell is going on? Are you bored?"

"Yeah, I'm bored—and tired," she said exhaling and wincing. "Ever go to that department store Marshall's?" she said enjoying her private joke with herself.

"No, not really. My wife does the shopping. My shopping is strictly online," he said.

"Marshall's not high-class enough for you?"

"Don't know. Never been there."

"Well, I was thinking about Marshall."

"What were you thinking?" he said looking directly into her eyes.

She turned her head as much as she could and said, "is that the best you can do?"

"Touché," he said when he realized how transparent his probing was.

"*Touché.* Do people ever really say that anymore?" she asked.

"If you were into fencing, I suppose you would."

"Are you into fencing?" she asked.

"No, are you?" he said, waiting for the punning to begin.

"I make good fences and good fences make good neighbors."

"Walling people in or walling people out?"

"Either way," she said.

"Is it hard to mend fences?"

"Think I'll take that other road less traveled by," she said. She was getting tired of the Robert Frost play on words.

"It'll make all the difference," he said.

"Barump bump," she said. She exhaled and was quiet.

"Retracing steps is pretty difficult when everything hurts," she continued.

"Especially when your heart does," he said. Damned she liked Noel. Too bad he was in psychiatry and not teaching English.

"You would have made a pretty good neighbor, Noel, fences or not."

He stroked her arm, gently, gently. He didn't want her to hurt any more than she was.

She thought of the plan she had for Marshall and herself.

"Oh, go on. You two enjoy your stroll in the hall alone. Marshall can have lunch with me," Ceci probably told Tracy and Stephanie.

"Can you manage and bring him to his mom's mini-van when you're done?" Tracy would ask.

"No prob."

Ceci wondered if she were the only one who was curious about Marshall's world. Was she the only one who was jealous and would do anything to be in it—with or without him? Oh, no, she couldn't get him started laughing that harpy laugh with its jagged, sharp edge which could cut away at the protective armor and into the soft tissue of her heart.

"Hey Marshall, my boy," she'd say. "You and I are going on a little trip. Would you like that?" Stretching however he could to see where Tracy and Stephanie went without him, he would then look at Ceci.

"First, we are going to lunch together here in my office. I'll take good care of you, okay?"

She prayed he'd laugh his Marshall laugh which was a wholehearted yes!

"Will you take good care of *me* and show me around?" she said. Marshall looked confused, but Ceci didn't wait for a response because there was no time. "Good," she'd mouth and wheel him to her office. She'd rummage through his book bag and take out the lunch his mother prepared and feed him however she could as he rolled his head back and forth. Or she'd let him feed himself and clean up the mess after him when he left. That was the least she could do.

Chapter 47

Jaime could never hide when she had been crying. Who could, Ceci thought. When Ceci was crying, she hated herself for not being able to conceal it. It was easy if someone phoned her. She was in much more control of her voice and it would pass for just a cold. But not so, in person. The puffiness in her eyes would need some time to go away. One hour, two hours and even then there were signs of heartache. Women were luckier, though, than men. They could put make-up on and cover sadness.

"Now don't tell me you have boyfriend trouble," she said to Jaime. "What gives? Why the puffy eyes? Was it something I said," Ceci said pouting.

Jaime was crying and didn't care if her mother watched. She cried to the point of sobbing.

"Ya can't go away, Mommy. What if we never see each other again? What will I do?"

Tim stroked his daughter's back and said to his wife, "It will get all straightened out, Cee. You just have to talk to Noel. Okay? Promise me you will talk to Noel."

"Noel Christian is a quack. Ph.D—Piled High and Deep. A charlatan. You know about quack shrinks, don't you Dr. McKinney?"

He didn't respond to the usual comments she used to make to him and his colleagues. He knew she never meant them. They merely were rebuttals to his jabs at educators, their overpay and their ten weeks of paid vacation.

"Oh, unlike the starving doctors who head one of the biggest psychiatric clinics in the country. Sorrrrrry," she'd say. They always used to laugh, but not today. Too much crying for laughing, she guessed. There were these slots in life: a laughing one and a crying one. Only one could be filled at a time with a person. You were either in one or the other. She could be in both.

With months of hospitalization for both her physical injuries as well as her emotional ones, Ceci could never fully mentally retrace her steps to the entrance of Marshall's world and couldn't remember if she, in fact, ever got there. She hoped she did.

Forced retirement had not been such a bad thing. Good pension. Prognosis of good physical health with which to enjoy it. It was lucky for her that her insurance would pay for someone to check up on her each day. It was also great that Tim could work from home. It was even better that he was allowed to treat her. Everything above board. Everything fit nicely into those square holes. Everything had a place in her house, especially the pills in the pill boxes with seven compartments, the initial of each day clearly stamped.

She didn't care that she didn't drive anymore. She didn't care that a special bus picked her up and brought her home. She liked that she could live in Marshall's world with him whenever she felt like—with an invitation or not.

She would be able to walk and balance one day, but she didn't care to. She didn't care that she couldn't talk because she didn't have anything to say. She didn't care that she could only move one arm as she was assured she would heal, but she didn't care to.

Chapter 48

Everyone had stopped at the entrance of Ceci's empty classroom. The room seemed quieter than normal. The lights were out, but they always were especially when Ceci was in her office. When the door was locked on her free period and the lights were out, everyone knew that Ceci was in the room. She knew that they knew it. That was okay because she needed that make-believe quiet, alone time. How could one be alone in a building with 1200 people all talking at the same time? All laughing at the same time? All walking at the same time? But, Ceci found a way to be absent from class. There was an enclosed courtyard near her office. The irony in that always amused her. If she did run into the courtyard, she would find herself in another cell with bells.

The only time they knew her room was empty was if the lights were on and the door was open. She thought nothing of leaving for the period with her pocketbook on top of her desk.

"Let them steal it. Who wants my stuff anyway?" she'd say to anyone who reminded her to at least lock up her bag. The contents of her pocketbook didn't reveal the real Ceci. Martin Luther King was right. What mattered were the contents of her heart. There, she thought, was a useless endeavor to tread on such uninhabited ground.

Tim and Alan were the only fools who tried to make that futile trek. Her heart was a wasteland where all the hollow men who lived there died with a whimper, not with a bang.

What would she have done without her literature? She would have no place to languish in the allusions except in the barrenness of her world. Certainly not in that empty chamber—at least with Poe there would be some rhyme or reason as in "The Raven" if it were indeed nevermore.

Principal Neil Jackson knew whose handbag it had been and checked to see what was missing. Can one see the nonexistence of something? The usual teacher things were in the bag, but there was no money in the wallet and there were no car keys. Where were they? In her blazer pocket?

"Jerry, did you see Mrs. McKinney leave the building?" Neil asked the custodian. Not wanting to get Ceci in any trouble because he liked her, he also was reluctant to disobey the principal.

"Yeah," Jerry said, "she looked like she was walkin' in her sleep or something. And then, all of a sudden, she ran out the side door."

The crossing guard did see an Infiniti go through a red light to get to the Seven-11 across the street. No, she didn't run out of the car, though. She just casually walked into the store. No, she didn't seem to have a handbag, but the guard didn't check so she couldn't be sure. The woman behind the counter in Seven-11 remembered Mrs. McKinney had no pocketbook because she was having a hard time remembering where she had put that damned coin purse. No it was just her keys that made the sound in her coat pocket. The money was loose in a pocket and there were enough bills in it to pay for the baby wipes.

"She still cracked me up," the cashier said. "But she looked like she was in a hurry and the funny thing was…"

"What was that?" the detective asked.

"Well, she said she was in a rush and then she just sat in the car for a real long time—like hours."

"What did she do after that?" the detective said getting annoyed at the cashier's lengthy account. "Did you go outside to see why she was sitting there? What was she doing?"

"Hey, my job is not to snoop into somebody else's business like yours is," she said.

"Okay. You have been very helpful ma'am. Thanks," the detective said controlling his desire to pour the hazelnut coffee over her head.

"Hey, that teacher ain't in no trouble is she? She's okay. She's cool."

"Thanks again. Be in touch," the detective said knowing what he had to do now.

Detective Reynolds always hated the duty of checking hospitals and worse, morgues. One woman was already admitted that afternoon with multiple fractures and apparently suffered from amnesia. He hated that amnesia stuff. Like whiplash. Everybody and his mother used that excuse. On that day, either excuse was true for Ceci. Wouldn't that just neatly wrap up the case, complete with ribbon of honesty and secured with cords of provable facts? Innocence neatly packed and easily portable, all to be filed in an antiseptic room of purity.

The hospital room smelled of alcohol.

"Phew. All ERs must be painted with that stuff," he said. Detective Reynolds was straight out of a Nelson DeMille novel. Reynolds *did* like DeMille cops, but would never verbalize this to his colleagues. He liked thinking people thought he was one of a kind. He tolerated DeMille books, but basically he hated to read cop stories because they never got it right. They were either crooked cops on the take or they were ultra ambitious, holier-than-thou ones. But they were the minority, he thought. They were the burnouts.

If teachers burned out, so what? Maybe a few kids would get away with razzing her; some grammar wouldn't have been taught; kids could peek at another kid's paper during a test and not get in trouble with the dean. What could happen if a teacher burned out?

He never thought of questioning Marshall.

Chapter 49

Ceci was still trying to recollect if she ultimately got into Marshall's world. She forced herself to imagine how she would have.

"Let's get on with it. Your face is so messy from that cup cake your mom gave you. I'll bet your sister packed your lunch."

Marshall's mom knew better. A Hostess chocolate cupcake was not what Mrs. Keller would have packed for him to maneuver with his one good hand. Even if a teacher wanted to help feed him, Marshall wouldn't allow it.

"Is it your pride, my dear boy? It's okay to have pride. Remember what I taught the class. Odysseus had hubris, pride. Nothing wrong with hubris as long as the qualities bragged about were true. Odysseus *was* strong, courageous, stalwart, brilliant. So, why shouldn't he boast? And you Marshall, you silly boy, you should have hubris because you are a hero in this physically fit functioning world of cowards."

She might have opened her closet and admired how she had made her room, especially this office section, so much like home. It was kind of like when CEOs had their own huge office and sectioned off a place to make it a suite. If they could take their place of business and convert part of it into an extension of an executive suite, why couldn't Ceci? Granted, she didn't have a bathroom or sink, but with the handicapped facilities directly next door to her, she enjoyed the privilege even though no other teachers were allowed. Those hall monitors were very diligent at making sure faculty used the faculty rest rooms. But not, Ceci. Mrs. McKinney could use it anytime she wanted to. She even had her own key.

She would search her well-stocked shelves, looking for some baby wipes and a towel. She'd wiped off the chocolatey mess from Marshall's mouth and dry his scrunched-up face with the white terry. She'd use the whole package of wipes and be angry that she couldn't clean him properly. She'd need to get more.

"Stand still Marshall. But you can't stand at all, can you," she'd say checking her dark humor.

"Marshall, don't get so upset. I will get us more wipes; don't worry. I will fix everything. And for heaven's sake don't try to talk. You know I can't understand you." She'd take a step back, fold her arms and say, "I'll just wait until you settle down. Such a handsome boy should be nice and clean when he takes a lady to his private world. What? You want to take me now?"

Ceci felt real terror and everything hit her as if she almost crashed through a windshield. Should she go with Marshall or get those damn wipes? Ceci could multi-task and would do both.

"Oh, oh. We're getting ready to take off. Wow, what a journey. Marshall, you really know how to live. I knew it. I knew it. I knew it. Good, don't say anything. Let me just take it all in." So much static. At least it was consistent static and nothing could intercept with annoying warnings which were beginning to vex her. Was this a car or an aircraft?

She was so impressed that her car had an automatic pilot.

Chapter 50

Ceci certainly knew how difficult it was to wheel Marshall around. She hoped Tim would appreciate it now.

"Serves you right, Timmy boy. Told you to build that entrance-way wider. All you had to do was build a walkway around the back yard from the front driveway to the sliding glass doors around back. But, noo. You never listen to me," she said. "Lucky for me I like sitting not too far from those nice wide double doors." She turned her attention to Marshall. "Why sir, you really look handsome. And how tall you got. Come here, let me look at you," she said to the empty side wall.

"Tim, would you wheel him closer to me?"

"Honey, I am preparing lunch. Give me a minute."

Jaime had decided that it would be a lot easier to realize her dream of independence and success by going to college. So she spent her senior year loading up on Advanced Placement courses taking college biology, English and Abnormal Psychology. She was sure she would ace the psych course with so much help from her mother. Ceci and the stress around the family seemed very far away when Jaime was deep into her books. Maybe Jimmy *was* the smarter of the two.

"Saves us a bundle of moolah. Paying for three years of college is a lot better than paying for four," Ceci had told Jaime when she excitedly told her parents she was accepted to Columbia.

And that Jimmy—James as he wanted to be called now—will get sick of living with Tim's brother, she thought.

"Uncle Marc is a lawyer, so what?"

"That's what I want to be, Mom."

"You can be a lawyer without having to live with one. That's like saying a doctor has to live with a patient. How dumb would that be?"

Ceci called Tim again.

"Cee, please be patient."

"But I *am* a patient," she said. "How hard is it to wheel Marshall to me?"

"Just relax, okay?"

"Sure, easy for you to say. You are nice and comfortable in your kitchen wearing that nerdy chef's apron with a picture of Freud along the bodice."

He had laughed so much when she was in her iron-on-clothing mode. She had scanned Freud's portrait from one of Tim's psych books, printed it out—good thing it was black and white, looked nicer transferred—and ironed it onto a white cookout chef's apron. It fit so nicely on the bib portion. And he always wore it with the bib over his head instead of the way the other husbands wore theirs, bibs folded down, apron tied only around the waist.

He waved to her from the kitchen, his reflection showing strain on his face as if she asked him to let Marshall in every day.

"Don't let me come over there," she said in her best wiseguy voice. She didn't really try to get up because she knew Tim would eventually let Marshall in. He could do many things at once. Tim was able to finish cooking and let that poor freezing, messy-faced child in without banging the wheelchair into the molding that Tim kept replacing and had been replacing since Ceci came home.

Tim's colleagues found it incredible that he still had patience to pacify his wife.

"There's nothing wrong with the molding," he'd say. Ceci's tense, wide-eyed stare of fright always got to him.

"Okay, okay. I'll change it." He needed only buy two interchangeable strips of molding because he would put the walnut up one week and replace it with the maple the next. This process could go on as long as Ceci could. And he counted on Ceci going on.

Ceci wanted to, but she dared not praise Tim. Not good for the character she would chuckle to herself. She did acknowledged how he could do two things at once and not miss a beat. In mere moments, he could get Marshall in and bring her lunch on a tray—all at precisely the same time.

It wasn't so bad, though. Marshall didn't visit so often and didn't stay too long. When he did come by, he didn't get messy, anymore. Tim probably cleaned him up. One of these days, Marshall would figure out that his Lotus Land was the same as Ceci's and he just might—one of these days—stay in hers.

It was an empty house now with her children gone. And it was good that Tim went bowling so often. His friends were not that bad after all.

It was only when the nurse was busy in the kitchen that Ceci allowed herself to cry for all the
　　Marshalls
　　grieving mothers
　　searching husbands and
　　damaged selves.